OUR LOVE
Unhinged

BRIGHTON WALSH

Edited by Ashley Turcotte of Brown Owl Editing
Cover Art © Brighton Walsh www.brightonwalsh.com

Our Love Unhinged is a work of fiction. Names, characters, places, and
incidents are either products of the author's imagination or are used
fictitiously, and any resemblance to actual persons, living or dead,
business establishments, events, or locales is coincidental.

Digital ISBN: 978-0-9971258-2-5
Paperback ISBN: 978-1-7338249-5-8
Special Edition Paperback ISBN: 978-1-68518-019-5

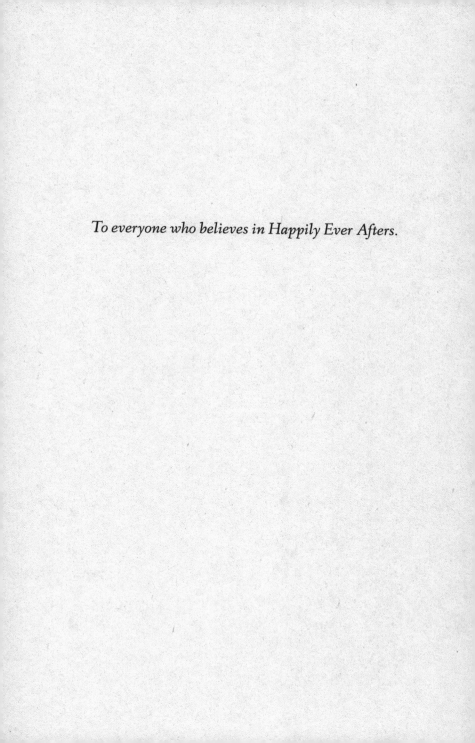

To everyone who believes in Happily Ever Afters.

ONE

March 5

winter

IT'S LATE, nearly midnight, by the time the front door opens, announcing Cade's arrival home from his closing shift at the restaurant. The light from the moon splashes across our bed as I lie waiting for him. Butterflies take flight in my stomach, the anticipation of seeing him in front of me enough to bring a grin to my face—one I can't even begin to suppress. My unfiltered, unrestrained smile—that I'd even *have* something to smile about—would've been so unusual only a couple years ago, it would've been comical.

Except I'm not that Winter anymore.

Through fights and arguments and anger and, yeah,

pain, there still hasn't been a single day without Cade putting a smile on my face at least once. When he came crashing into my life those years ago, he brought his light until it was fused into every part of me, filling up my emptiness and shadows.

The feeling creeping up from my toes is one I'm not sure I'll ever get used to—something I never expected to feel at all. Contentment. Happiness. Pure, utter bliss.

All thanks to the changes spurred on in my life by one man.

His keys hit the counter somewhere in the kitchen, and then there's shuffling—probably him shedding his chef's coat and slipping off his shoes. And then before I can blink, Cade's massive shoulders blot out nearly all the light from the hall as he stands in the doorway to our bedroom. *Our* bedroom. And holy shit, how did I get this lucky? That he opened up his family home to me, did everything he could to make it my home too, is more than I could've ever hoped for. It's more than I ever thought I'd be lucky enough to experience. More than I ever thought I deserved.

And just like always, I'm enraptured by that stare. His hazel eyes stay locked with mine for a moment, until he breaks the connection and makes a slow perusal down my body. I'm not wearing anything sexy, just my normal nightly uniform—one of his old, discarded shirts and a pair of panties—but from the way his gaze heats, his tongue sneaking out to lick a path across his full bottom lip, I might as well be in a see-through nightie.

Without words, he lifts his gaze to me as he walks

toward the bed, shedding his clothes until he's wearing nothing but the look of hunger on his face. His desire wraps around me like a blanket, surrounding me in heat. I can feel it from my head all the way to my toes, can feel it seeping into my very *bones*.

How is it like this? How is it *still* like this? I thought it would wane somehow. That in the months and years since we've been together, this spark between us would fizzle out, fade until it became boring and stale. That this all-over ache wouldn't still consume me after hundreds and hundreds of days.

But as he climbs onto the foot of the bed, picking up my left ankle and bringing it to his lips, I can't imagine not feeling this *pull* toward him. And with the way his eyes won't stray from mine, with the way he practically worships me with his mouth and hands, his rough finger-tips running up and down my leg, I'm secure in the fact that it's the same for him.

"How was work?" I manage through a gasp as his lower lip finds the sensitive skin behind my knee.

Cade makes a sound low in his throat but doesn't answer. Instead, he continues on his path, his lips trailing up up up my leg until he's nearly where I want him. I shift my hips, lifting my ass off the bed and presenting myself to him like an offering. He just breathes out a laugh, the puffs of air ghosting over where I'm hot and so ready for him, and then switches sides and moves to the other leg.

On an exhale, I drop my hips to the bed, knowing he's not going to give in easily. This is a game we play every night he works late. He comes home, the adrenaline of a good dinner service still pumping through his veins, practically rolling off him, and it's all he can do to grunt a few words before he needs to be inside me.

And because I'm just as desperate for him by the time I see all that focused energy solely on me—*for* me—I do what I can to speed things up. Like encourage him to put my mouth to better uses than pestering him with questions. "Did your new sous chef start today?"

His only answer is an openmouthed kiss that lands on my right ankle, then my calf, my knee, the inside of my thigh, just inches from the seam of my underwear.

"How did everyone like your new entrée?" The question is a panted mess because he's hovering just over the barely there excuse for panties I'm wearing and I can't *think.*

He looks up at me from between my legs, parted to accommodate his wide shoulders. And by the gleam in his eyes, I know I've finally pushed him exactly where I want him. "If you're still this coherent, I'm not doing something right. Let me see if I can figure out how to make sure the only words coming out of your mouth are, Oh God, Cade, faster, more, and yes."

My fingers are restless at my sides, clutching and unclutching the sheets, my body coiled tightly as it waits for what it knows is coming. "What about fuck?"

The tiniest smile curves one side of his mouth. "That works, too." And then he pulls my panties off before his fingers slide up and down through all my wetness. I barely have time to blink before his mouth is on me, devouring me like he hasn't had me in days, weeks, months, when in fact it's been mere hours. I can't see, can't breathe, can't do anything but move my hands to his head, rubbing my fingers over the rough velvet of his close-cropped hair, and hold him to me, willing to go wherever he plans to take me.

Always.

He's relentless in his pursuit of my climax, working me up faster than I expected, and when he sucks my clit into his mouth, his tongue fluttering against it at the same time, I fall. I arch off the bed, a silent scream falling from my mouth as I pulse against his lips, riding out the wave of my intense orgasm. I'm still breathing heavily, my eyelids drooping, when he covers my body with his, fists his cock, and guides himself inside me.

"Cade, God . . ." I say, reaching down and digging my nails into his ass, pulling him deeper.

"Those are the kinds of words I like to hear." His thrusts are slow and deep, his hips rolling against me.

And while it's good—it's *always* good—I want all that built up adrenaline to come out in the way he's fucking me. I want him to be as lost with me as I always am with him.

I lift my thighs higher on his hips, clench my inner walls around his thick length, and pull his head down toward me. With fluttering brushes of my lips against his ear, I whisper, "I want you incoherent, too."

He drops his forehead to my neck on an exhale, his whole body shuddering before he pulls away, sitting back on his heels. With my legs hooked over his arms and his hands braced on the small of my back, he lifts me up into his lap as if I weigh no more than a rag doll. The muscles in his arms bunch and tighten under his tattoos as he moves me over him, lifting me up and down on his cock, his breath puffing against my mouth. "Baby, you know I'm already gone over you."

No matter how many times we're together, this feeling of complete and utter *belonging* never goes away. It's in the tenderness of Cade's touch, how his fingertips trail up and down my spine, even as he's driving deep inside me. It's woven in the soft cadence of his voice as he whispers my name, telling me I'm beautiful and sexy and that he craves my touch when he's not here. It's sparked in his eyes when he looks at me as he holds me above him, slowly working us both toward our climaxes.

"Missed you," he says, rolling his hips up into me as he lets me sink down on him, showing me he's got nowhere else to be. Showing me I'm it. *This* is it.

It's everything.

Pulled taut from the feelings he's wringing from my body, I breathe out a laugh. "You've been gone for twelve hours."

He brushes his lips along my jaw, his voice a quiet rumble. "And I missed you every single one of them."

"Oh, jeez." Outside, I roll my eyes, but inside . . . inside, I'm dying a little. While Cade and I have been together now for two years, it's not hard to remember the twenty-two years before that when no one wanted me, not even my mother. And to know this man—this amazing, thoughtful, intelligent, sexy man—wants me? *Loves* me?

It's unexplainable.

He holds me still above him, not giving either of us the movements we want. Instead, he swoops in and sucks my bottom lip into his mouth, releasing it with a pop. "You're sure chatty while you're supposed to be blissed out of your mind. Am I boring you? Losing my touch? This is the second time tonight. Maybe I need to spend some time on Paige's Tumblr and get some new moves."

This time I let out a full laugh, my head falling back, my arms braced against his shoulders. The fact that he even asked that question is absurd, and he knows it. That's proven when his teeth scrape against the column of my neck as he snaps his hips up, driving his length deep inside me. I can't help the surprised gasp that's pulled from my mouth. Then he tilts my hips forward just enough so his cock hits the perfect spot every time he thrusts—the spot he knows exactly how to reach. I dig my fingernails into his shoulders, my eyelids fluttering closed as I moan toward the ceiling.

"There we go. Stay with me, baby."

If he'd have me, I'd stay right here forever.

Cade slips a hand under my shirt until he has a handful of my breast, his thumb running back and forth, back and forth, over my nearly-too-sensitive nipple. "Get this off," he says, trying to shove the shirt over my head with one hand and keeping our bodies rocking together with the other. "Much as I love you in my clothes, I need to get my mouth on these perfect tits."

I whip the shirt off and grab the back of his neck, moaning his name against the top of his head when he sucks one nipple into his mouth. He moves his attention to my other breast, flicking his tongue against the hard tip, before brushing kisses across my chest, my collarbone, my shoulders, up my neck as he keeps our rhythm smooth and relaxed. He rests his forehead against mine, and I can't do anything but hold on as he rides me with meaning . . . with intention.

Cade's worked my body over so many times, has brought me to a thousand orgasms, that he knows what I need to get there almost better than I know myself. And it's like he's made it his mission to show me exactly that, especially when his grip on my ass tightens, his fingers digging into my flesh. How he pulls out slowly, then snaps his hips up fast, making me pant against his mouth, breathing him in as our bodies work toward our peaks together.

"Close, baby," he says, slipping a hand between us as he presses his thumb to my clit, and that's all I need to see stars. He groans, rocking harder into me, his cock pulsing deep inside me as I clench around him. And as he holds me close to him, my name a prayer on his lips, his arms locked tightly around me, I know he's giving me everything he has.

Every night after work, he's exhausted. I can see it in his eyes, in the way he carries himself. But when he comes home, he still gives me *everything*. Just like always. He'd bleed himself dry for me if I let him.

But that's the difference between me now and me two years ago . . . I'm willing to bleed myself dry for him, too. I'm willing to give him all of me—every crazy, screwed up piece—because we work. What we have together now is perfect.

And I don't ever want it to change.

March 6

cade

IT'S 2 a.m. and I'm wide awake, looking down at a sleeping Winter, her eyes fluttering under closed lids. She's curled into my side, her cheek resting on my chest, one of her legs thrown over mine—the same position she's in every night. My T-shirt is once again covering all those perfect curves and smooth skin, but I don't even care. Her cold toes are pressed against my calves, and I wouldn't have it any other way. This girl could crook her finger at me, and I'd be at her side in a millisecond. I'm so far gone, it'd be laughable if it wasn't so fucking perfect—if *we* weren't so fucking perfect.

As quietly as I can, I reach over and open the drawer of my bedside table, pulling out the small square box before placing it on my chest, not two inches from Winter's parted lips. I run my thumb over the smooth velvet before lifting the lid and staring at the ring that took me months to find—the perfect blend of beauty, timelessness, and simplicity. The lady who sold it to me called it an antique Art Deco ring. All I know is it looks like something Winter will love. Small, but not too small, nontraditional, and absolutely beautiful.

I have the perfect ring and the perfect girl. Now I just need the perfect proposal.

And that goddamn proposal has been a thorn in my side since the day I walked home with the ring. I've carried this box with me everywhere we've gone for the past three months. On every trip to the movies, every dinner out, every afternoon with the group, every babysitting trip to watch Haley. To the mall, on walks around the neighborhood, to the fucking grocery store. I've just about popped the question a dozen times, but every time, the words get stuck in my throat and I choke.

Because what if it's not everything she thought it'd be?

She's dealt with an abundance of shit in her life, has overcome so much to become the amazing woman she is, and I want this to be perfect for her, too. She *deserves* this to be perfect for her.

I want it to be a story she's proud to someday tell our kids and grandkids.

And the thing of it is, Winter probably wouldn't care if I asked her when she was fresh out of the shower, me sitting propped on the vanity in the bathroom. Or if I made a pizza and spelled out *will you marry me* in pepperoni slices. She wouldn't care if it was done at the top of the Eiffel Tower or in our backyard.

She absolutely wouldn't care, and I don't want to wait another fucking minute without knowing if she'll be my wife.

That realization pours gasoline on the fire that's been a slow burn for the past three months as I tried to find the perfect setting, causing this feeling inside to turn into an inferno. There *is* no perfect setting. There's just me and her and this amazing love I'm somehow lucky enough to be part of. And I can't wait—I don't *want* to wait anymore.

I reach over and switch on the bedside lamp, then turn back to her and squeeze her hip, pulling her closer and brushing my lips against her forehead. "Baby? Baby, wake up."

She shifts as I run my hand up and down her side, and I roll so we're lying face to face. Her eyes flutter open and she smiles the softest smile at me before her eyelids droop again.

I run my thumb back and forth on her jaw, kissing both her eyelids. "Winter. Wake up. I have something I need to ask you."

"Now?" she mumbles, her face turned into the pillow.

"Yes, now."

"What time's it?"

"Time for you to wake up. Baby, please. Open your eyes."

She does as I ask, her eyelids slowly blinking open, and then she's staring at me through half-closed eyes. Until, somehow, the ring catches her attention, and her eyes widen as she stares at it. Her mouth drops open, her fingers hovering over her lips. When she finally lifts her gaze to me, a hundred questions swarm in those grayish-green depths. It feels like the weight of a car lifts off my shoulders, knowing I don't have to wait anymore.

"I've been walking around with this in my pocket for three months, waiting for the perfect time to ask you. But the problem with striving for perfection is that every day I was waiting for the perfect setting and the perfect words and the perfect time was just another day further away from making you my wife. And I just can't fucking wait any longer. I want you to be with me, Winter. Today until forever."

She opens her mouth, then shuts it, her fingers pressing against her lips before she tentatively reaches out and brushes them against the velvet of the box. "You already have me. Today until forever. I don't need a ring to tell me that."

"Humor me."

Shaking her head, she breathes out a laugh. "Humor me—now there's your perfect proposal." Her voice is just as shaky as her hand, and I know she's probably freaking out, but I can read everything I need to in her eyes—how they're lit up with excitement and happiness.

I stroke the outside of her hand with my thumb as I grip the box in front of me. "Okay, you need a perfect proposal? How about this: I can't live another day without knowing you'll be my wife. Please don't make me. Say yes, baby."

She presses her lips together, her fingertips continuing to brush back and forth along the small box as she stares at the ring. When she still doesn't say anything, I start to worry maybe the ring I thought was something that matched her personality exactly doesn't at all, and she hates it.

Swallowing, I say, "I know it's not very traditional. I didn't think you'd want a diamond, but we can get something different if you don't—"

"I love it."

I breathe out a sigh of relief. "Okay."

"Okay."

Lifting both eyebrows, I repeat, "Okay? Is that a yes? Because you haven't said much, and I kinda just ripped my heart out and dropped it at your feet."

She's quiet for another moment, then she whispers, "Are you sure you want to do this?"

I move an arm around to her back and press our bodies together, letting her feel exactly how much I want it. I've been rock fucking solid since I decided I was going to do this tonight, adrenaline and excitement shooting straight to my cock. "This is what the thought of you wearing my ring does to me. So yeah, I want to do this. Can't say there's much else I'd *rather* do."

"Cade . . ." She looks up at me, then reaches out, wrapping her arms tightly around my neck, the box getting smashed between us. I run my hand up and down the length of her back, holding her to me, and I'm not sure if it's her or me who's shaking—maybe both of us. But then her lips move against the shell of my ear, a soft, "Yes," coming out of her mouth, and it doesn't matter.

She's mine. Today until forever.

TWO

March 6

winter

I STRETCH and reach toward Cade's side of the bed, finding nothing but cool sheets where his furnace of a body normally is. I blink open my eyes and look at the bright red numbers proclaiming 10:37 a.m. The late time would normally be enough to jolt me out of bed, since we have less than half an hour before everyone will be here for our weekly Sunday brunch. But the brand new piece of jewelry on my left hand, glinting in the sunlight streaming in through the windows, stops me cold.

Oh shit.

Oh *shit*.

That wasn't a dream. Cade waking me up in the middle of the night because he couldn't stand to wait another minute before I agreed to be his wife. Him slipping the ring on my finger before taking me hard and fast, then pumping his cock inside me until he was hard enough to take me again, that time slow and sweet while he whispered how good he was going to be to me, how I'd never have to worry about anything as his wife, how he'd always work to make me happy.

I'd fallen asleep in his arms not worried about him doing that for me—like I'd ever be worried about that with Cade. Instead, I'd worried about whether or not *I'd* be able to do that for *him* every day for the rest of our lives.

He picks that moment to come strolling into the room wearing nothing but a too-small towel clutched together with a hand at his hip. "Morning, baby," he says with a smile. "All the bath sheets are dirty, so I had to make do with one of your Barbie towels. How do people even use these?" He gestures to the way his large, muscled thigh hangs out between the gaping sides of the towel, but he freezes the second his eyes lift to mine.

There must be something that alerts him to trouble—possibly the way I'm breathing like I'm about to have a panic attack or maybe how I've gone as white as the sheets I'm lying on while I divide my attention between him in that ridiculously tiny towel and the beautiful and, yeah, perfect, ring on my finger—because he's at my side in a second, minuscule towel long forgotten.

He brushes the hair away from my face. "How much time do we have before you freak out?"

They're practically the same words he said to me nearly two years ago, the first time we slept together on my stupid, shitty futon, and I almost laugh. But how can I when that just reminds me of where I came from and how far I truly have to go to be even remotely worthy of a man like Cade?

"That didn't get the laugh I thought it would. Damage control it is." He rolls over me until I'm caged under him. My hands are curled against my chest, and he leans down and presses his lips to the ring he gave me last night. "You can take it back if you want to. I'd *like* you to wear my ring, but I don't need you to. I'd want you to be my wife, ring or not."

The thought of me having to give this up splits my heart in half. I'd like to wear his ring, too, and not just because it'd make him happy. Because it'd make *me* happy to see that sign of his love on my body every single day. But I can't deny that it terrifies the ever-loving shit out of me. Does he even know what he's doing, tying himself to me for the rest of his life?

Without taking my eyes off the emerald cut sapphire surrounded by tiny, sparkling diamonds, I whisper whatever truth I can give him. "I . . . I kind of don't want to. Take it off."

He watches me, *reads* me, and then nods, like he knows exactly what I'm thinking. "And that scares you?"

Turns out he *does* know exactly what I'm thinking.

I swallow, looking up into his eyes—eyes that are gazing down at me with nothing but openness and acceptance. "A little." My response causes him to quirk an eyebrow, and I huff out a laugh. "Okay, a lot."

Bringing his hands to cradle my head, he rubs his thumbs in soothing circles against my temples, and I have no idea how I can feel so safe and so utterly panicked at the same time. "I get that it scares you," he says. "I'd be shocked if it didn't. But that's not all you're feeling . . . right?"

I shake my head, but I can't say anything. How could I possibly put into words how I feel about him? How I feel about *us*? How I feel about the idea of us being bound to each other for the rest of our lives? That it feels as vast and overwhelming and beautiful and *terrifying* as being on the beach, watching the power and beauty of the ocean as it surges and roars minutes before a tidal wave strikes.

"Do you want this, Winter?" he asks. "Do you want to be with me for the rest of your life?"

The answer pours from my lips before I can even stop to consider it. "Of course. *Of course.*"

His smile is as blinding as it is genuine, and he swoops down to kiss me, his lips moving against mine as he says, "Then we'll figure everything else out as we go."

He's said that to me a dozen times before, and that's part of the problem. I'm so damn tired of constantly being the one holding us back. Of being the one who always puts up a fight, hesitates instead of jumping straight in where Cade's concerned. He's so patient . . . so kind and understanding. He never pushes me. He accepts every bit of me, including the fucked up pieces I wish I could escape, if only for a moment. But the thing is, they're always going to be with me, even if they're just lurking in the corners, buried under months of happiness and contentment. They're always going to be there, waiting to float to the surface, because they're a part of me, and nothing will change that. Not even Cade.

And yet he's always there to pull me back, to talk me down, to convince me or reassure me. To make me feel loved and wanted and needed.

But, *God*, how is that fair to him? How many times should he have to be there, waiting to pick up my pieces when I fall apart?

I stuff those worries down, bury them deep because I don't want them to be displayed all over my face. I don't want him to even consider that I don't want this—don't want *him*.

He watches me for a minute, his thumbs still rubbing soothing circles against my head. "You feel better, baby? Want me to call everyone and cancel for this week?"

I'm shaking my head before I even get any words out. "No. I don't want to cancel. Haley's going to practice her dance for us, remember?"

"I remember, but we can see it some other time if you need a while before we tell everyone."

My pulse kicks up a notch, but I swallow down my nerves and paste on a smile. One he can see right through if the look on his face and the way he narrows his eyes are any indication. "No, today is fine. But maybe you can put some pants on first. Not that I'm complaining."

He doesn't say anything for a moment, his eyes darting between mine and gauging me, just like he's done a hundred times before. "You say the word, and I'll kick everyone out. We can spend all day in bed if you want. Just you and me."

"If *I* want? I think you have that backward."

He drops his lower body into the cradle of my thighs and makes a slow, concentrated roll of his hips, the head of his naked cock pressing against my slit through my thin, cotton underwear. My eyes flutter back in my head, and I breathe out his name. Three times last night, and he can still make my body sing with nothing more than a grazing touch.

"Mhmm . . ." he says against my neck, the scruff on his face rasping against my skin. "Like you're not dying to have my mouth on you again."

There's no use denying it because it has to be written all over my face, not to mention the way I lift my hips to meet his.

"That's what I thought," he says before he steals a kiss, then he's off me and walking toward the dresser. His ass is sculpted perfection, enough to distract me from the fact that my soon-to-be sister-in-law—oh *God*—will be here in fifteen minutes, and I'm still mostly naked from our middle-of-the-night activities.

Cade slides a pair of gray boxer briefs over all that perfection, then snags a pair of cargo shorts and pulls them on, leaving his chest bare. A few water droplets trace the lines of the tattoos covering his arms, others just hanging out in the hills and valleys created by his ridiculous muscles. After grabbing a T-shirt from a drawer, he shoots me a smile over his shoulder. "Show's over, baby. Go hop in the shower and come out when you're ready."

He could've phrased that a dozen different ways—come out when I'm done, or in twenty minutes, or when I hear all the commotion that follows our friends when they enter—but he didn't. He knows me so fucking well, knows I need time to get my shit together. Knows I need time to get used to things, and considering I thought last night was a dream, I've had all of seven minutes to let the idea settle that Cade asked me to be his wife and I said yes.

But it doesn't matter . . . I can't let it. I said yes, and I meant it. Besides that, I don't want to be the one who holds us back anymore.

I just hope my *want* is strong enough to force it into existence.

cade

HOW MUCH LONGER AM I supposed to keep this shit locked up? Is there some kind of rule? A code I'm supposed to follow? The truth is, I've been ready to blow for the past four months, since the day I started looking for rings. I haven't told a single person—didn't think it'd be right. It was for Winter and me only, and I *wanted* it to be all ours.

But now? Knowing she's twenty feet away in our bedroom, getting dressed while wearing my ring? Jesus. I want to climb onto the roof and shout it to the world. Winter Jacobson is going to be my *wife*. She's going to be by my side for the rest of my life. How did I ever get so damn lucky?

It's cold as hell outside, so we're all packed into the dining room, everyone talking at once. But I can't pay attention to any of it, because Winter's not out here yet. Maybe she's more freaked out than I thought. It seemed like she relaxed after our talk, but maybe it did jack shit, and she's in there right now trying to figure out a way to come out here without her ring on and not hurt my feelings. Maybe she's already bolted out the bathroom window just to be able to breathe.

Before I can go check on her, suddenly she's there, her still-wet hair piled on top of her head, a pencil stabbed through the middle of the messy knot to keep it in place. It's the same way she wears it when she's hard at work coding a site or when she's in the kitchen with me as I try to teach her how to make a dish. The same way that drives me fucking crazy because it shows off her long neck and collarbones. And that feeling is only amplified now as one side her sweater slips off, baring a shoulder. I had her three times last night, and I still want to kick everyone out, toss all this food from the table, and have her for breakfast instead.

"Oh thank Christ," Jase mumbles, too low for Haley to hear. Then louder, "I was about to start eating my napkin."

"Sorry, guys. I got up late."

"I just bet you did," Paige says, leering and wiggling her eyebrows at Winter.

Winter rolls her eyes but laughs. She glances at the table, then goes into the kitchen and comes back with both the apple and orange juices. Conversation continues around us, but it's just garbled sounds to me as I hold my breath, waiting for her to sit down. As she does so, she reaches out and sets the juices on the table, and I spot her ring, my entire body relaxing as a breath whooshes out.

"*What is that?*" Tessa's voice has risen four octaves, her eyes wide as she extends a finger to point at Winter's left hand.

Winter snatches her hand back and folds them together on her lap, glancing at me out of the corner of her eye.

"Oh, no. No, no, no, you can't hide it. Oh my God, oh my *God*! Is that an engagement ring? Are you getting *married*?" Tessa's voice has only managed to get higher pitched the more words that come out of her mouth, and she's moved to a standing position, her upper body nearly folded over the table as she tries to see Winter's hand.

"Calm down, sister," Paige says, tugging her down to sit, but she can't hide the curiosity in her eyes as she divides her attention between Winter and me.

"Nah, that's not an engagement ring," Jase says, totally unaffected as he dishes up a plate for Haley and then for himself. "He would've asked me to help him pick it out." He freezes as he reaches for the OJ for Haley. "Unless you asked Adam and not me." He narrows his eyes at me, then darts them to Adam, who holds up his hands.

"I know nothing about a ring," Adam says.

Jase makes a decisive nod, then pours Haley her juice. "See? Not an engagement ring."

Winter looks over at me, the ring in question being twisted around and around on her finger. She's nervous. That much is obvious. Even though I've done everything I could over the past two years to show her this little family of mine is *her* family, too, she still feels out of place. Though that's to be expected when you've got five people who've known each other most of their lives. Still, I want her to be comfortable with this, with all of it, so I'm going to let her do whatever she needs to do, as much as I want to put a spotlight on her hand. I reach out and squeeze her knee, letting her know I'll follow her lead.

But instead of letting the question pass and dishing up some breakfast, she clears her throat and brings her hand up from under the table, holding it out for everyone to see. "Actually, it is. An engagement ring."

A chorus of reactions go off around us, Haley clapping and squealing about getting to wear a flower girl dress, Paige and Tessa fawning over the ring, Jase bitching about the fact that I didn't even tell him I was thinking of doing this while Adam claps a hand on my shoulder, his quiet approval evident.

Even with all the commotion, all I can pay attention to

is Winter's face as she listens to my sister babble on about dresses and flowers and invitations. She looks happy, but there's no denying the undercurrent of uncertainty and nerves. But even so, she did this. She opened up about our plans, put herself at the mercy of my overly exuberant sister when she probably would've liked a couple days to get used to the idea first. And she did all that for me. I didn't have to say a word for her to know how much I wanted to tell my family, how much I wanted to share this with them. She just simply did it because she knew it'd make me happy.

And that right there is why I'll love her every day for the rest of my life, until I take my dying breath. And why I'll spend every single one of them trying to make her as happy as she makes me.

THREE

April 21

winter

I BLOW the hair out of my face as I divide my attention between the recipe I searched for on Pinterest and the pan on the stove. I have no fucking idea how Cade manages to do this day in and day out. And not just *this*—this tiny meal for two. Oh, no. He makes dinner for hundreds of people a night like it's no big deal. When he cooks something for just the two of us, he does it with the level of ease I could only replicate by using Haley's Easy-Bake Oven to make him less-than-mediocre brownies.

I'm no stranger to the kitchen. My life never afforded me the luxury of being able to eat out, so I know my way around. But I know things like how long to boil packaged noodles and how to hit a jar just right to get it to open. Granted, maybe a made-from-scratch Italian meal for my chef boyfriend—*fiancé*—whose specialty happens to be Italian wasn't my smartest idea, but it is what it is. Too late to go back now.

Besides that, I wanted to do *something*. It's been a month and a half since he first put this ring on my finger, and I can't stop the worry niggling me—that I need to try and prove my worth. I haven't said that to him, because he'd shit a brick. Still, I can't help what I'm feeling, and right now . . . these past several weeks . . . I've felt inadequate, to say the least.

It's not as if there's been a sudden influx of insecurities. They've always been there, but they were far enough under the surface that I was able to ignore them. Just go about our lives as if they didn't exist. But that all went up in smoke the day he asked to share *all* my days. The day he asked to be tied down to me. He's only known me for two years, and we've only been officially together for a year and a half of that. How can he possibly know he wants to spend his *life* with me?

Our whole relationship, Cade has been the rock, so firm and steadfast in his commitment to me. He's been the one holding us together when I thought for sure we'd fall apart. I give him my love and myself, but how can that be enough when he gives me *everything*?

So, yeah, a homemade dinner might seem inconsequential—like throwing a pebble into the Grand Canyon—

but if I can do this . . . if I can make him a stupid meal, maybe I won't be the horrible wife my recurring nightmares tell me I will be. And those nightmares haven't left me alone since he placed this ring on my finger. The one I hate the most—and, naturally, the one I have the most often—is when he abandons me in the ice cream aisle of a supermarket, like my mom did. Just walks away and never looks back.

I try to shake the heaviness settling over me and glance at the clock as I stir the more-brown-than-red sauce, wrinkling my nose. It doesn't look or smell like the amazing stuff Cade normally makes, but I only have twenty minutes before he'll come through that door, so there's no time to start over. I want him to walk in from his more than twelve hours at the restaurant and be able to sit down and enjoy dinner instead of hurrying to whip up something exquisite for us like he does whenever he doesn't close at the restaurant. Just once, I want to ease the burden and do something for *him*.

Fifteen minutes later, I'm covered in flour, the pasta dough is an absolute fucking disaster, and then to top it all off, the fire alarm goes off . . . just as Cade walks through the door.

"Shit!" Abandoning the ruined pasta, I rush over to the oven, coughing as I wave the smoke away with a potholder and pull out the charred pieces of garlic bread. And doesn't that black, crusty bread just about sum up this whole godawful attempt at dinner? After carrying the pan over to the sink, I drop everything inside, the bread sliding down into the ceramic basin. I rest my hands on the counter and let out a long breath, my head dropping between my shoulders.

The fire alarm cuts off, no doubt thanks to Cade. He probably reached up and plucked it right from the ceiling. The sliding back door cracks open, and then Cade comes closer. I haven't lifted my head, can't stand to see pity—or worse, revulsion—on his face, but I can feel him. His presence raises the fine hairs on the back of my neck, and that feeling only amplifies as he comes up behind me, his hands resting on top of mine on either side of me. The hard planes of his body fit against my back as he presses his nose into my neck and inhales deeply.

"What's all this?" he asks.

I'm too tired to even try to say anything but the truth. "It's my failed attempt at the practice run for being the perfect wife."

I expect a lot of reactions from him, but his bark of laughter isn't one of them. He guffaws so loud and so long that my spine straightens in response. I'm rigid and unmoving in front of him, and he must finally realize it, because his laughter cuts off and he turns me around to face him. My eyes are downcast, my arms crossed against my chest, but my closed-off body language doesn't deter him.

"Winter." He squeezes my sides, trying to get me to look at him.

I studiously ignore him, looking off to the side instead of at him. It's stupid and childish, but I can't help it—not when he just laughed at me. I don't know if he was laughing at my attempt at dinner or over the fact that I thought I could even *be* the perfect wife, but it doesn't matter. It stings all the same.

"Baby . . ." This time he ducks his head until he snags my attention. "I wasn't laughing. I'm sorry."

"No? What was all that noise coming out of your mouth?"

"Okay, I was laughing, but not at *you*."

"Seriously? You're going with the, 'I wasn't laughing *at* you but *with* you' argument?"

"No, that's not what I'm doing. I was laughing at the fact that you thought I'd even *want* a perfect wife." He must feel me stiffen even further, because he wraps his arms around me to keep me from ducking under his arm and storming into the bedroom like I want to. "Don't get pissed off. Just hear me out." He pulls back and looks at me, one eyebrow lifted. "You gonna listen?"

"Say what you're going to say so I can decide if this sauce goes on your plate or in your lap."

His smile starts out slow, just a quirk of his lips, until it sweeps over his face. "That right there is why I'd never want a perfect wife. You think a perfect wife would threaten to dump pasta sauce in my lap?"

I groan and drop my forehead to his chest. "Oh God, I'm failing before I even have the job."

His chest rumbles with a laugh as he runs his hands up and down my back. "You're not failing. And what the hell makes you think I'd want anything but who you *are*? Have I made you feel like that?"

"God no," I say quickly, not wanting him to think any of this falls on his shoulders. It's all me. It always is. "I was just . . ." I blow out a long breath. "I just wanted to do something nice for you. Cook for you so you could have one night off. Isn't that what good almost-wives do?"

"I don't know about any other almost-wives. I only know about *you*. And I don't give a shit if you never cook anything for me, because that's what *I* do, okay? I love feeding you."

"But that's my point. You do all this stuff for me. What can I do for you? Build you a website?" I scoff and roll my eyes, even though my face is still pressed to the cotton covering his chest, hidden from his view.

"What can you do for me? You think anyone else picks up my favorite candy on their way home just because? Or sends me silly texts to make my days go by faster? Or would go to a movie they hated just because they know it's my favorite? Nobody else hangs around to clean up the mess I make after I cook or tries out weird food combinations because I had a wild idea—that's all you. Our relationship can't fit into a nice, neat package, baby. We don't do things perfectly around here, remember? We've tried hard to figure out what works for us, and we're there. I don't know why you'd think I'd want to change it. Or why I'd suddenly want someone other than who you are."

He's right. Of course he is. We've gone through a lot of trial and error while we figured out what worked for us and what didn't. Where we each fit into this relationship and the roles we took on—conventional or not. But this weight still rests on my shoulders, and I'm not sure it'll ever leave. I'm glad I haven't yet lifted my face from his chest, because it's going to be a lot easier to say this without having to look at him.

"I just . . ." I swallow and press closer to his beating heart, my hands grasping fistfuls of his shirt. I let his familiar scent surround me as I take a deep breath, then whisper, "I want to be worthy of your love, and I don't know that I'll ever be."

He freezes for a second, his entire body going taut, his hands pausing in their caresses on my back. "Baby . . ." His voice is hoarse, the single word coming out like a broken plea. He wraps his arms around me and easily lifts me onto the countertop so we're eye to eye, his hips settled between my legs. "Why would you *ever* worry about that?"

"Why *wouldn't* I?"

He shakes his head and brings his hand up to my neck, his thumb running along my jaw. "That's *my* job. It's what I worry about every day, what I work for."

I'm so stunned he could possibly think that when he's everything to me, I can only manage to repeat what he already said. "Why would you *ever* worry about that?"

Leaning in, he presses a kiss against one corner of my mouth, then the other. He cradles my jaw in his hands, and then his lips are against mine, soft and sweet, just the barest brush of his tongue. After a few moments, he pulls back and rests his forehead on mine, his eyes still closed. "Why *wouldn't* I?"

His words settle over me, the honesty of them seeping into my soul. Never in a million years would I have thought Cade would worry about that. Worry about being worthy of *me*? It's laughable.

Is that how he feels, too? When he heard that I worried about it, did he think I was crazy, the same way I thought of him? We can see it so clearly in each other, but agonize about it in ourselves. Knowing I'm not alone in this eases the pressure on my shoulders, ever so slightly.

"Know what else you do for me that no one else does?" he asks.

"What?"

The grin he shoots me is one hundred percent devil, mischief sparking in his eyes. He reaches back, shutting off the oven and the burner on the stove. Then I'm over his shoulder, one of his hands gripping my ass as he carries me into the bedroom, where he shows me exactly what I do for him that no one else does.

Twice.

FOUR

May 10

cade

THAT PLACE we just visited was a lot of things, but *bakery* sure as shit wasn't one of them. I don't even pause as I walk through the side door of the house and storm into the kitchen, Winter trailing behind me. My mom's old recipe box is down from the cupboard in three seconds flat, and I'm shuffling through the contents as I look for her vanilla cake recipe.

"Are you seriously doing this?" Winter pulls out a stool at the island and takes a seat.

"Those hacks aren't making our wedding cake. Who the fuck doesn't use vanilla beans in *vanilla bean* frosting?

Who? People who have no business in a kitchen, that's who."

"And you think you're going to have time to whip up a cake the day before the wedding, is that it?"

"If that's what I have to do to ensure no one else has to suffer through that dry, crumbly, flavorless disgrace of a mess, then yes."

"You don't bake," Winter says. "In fact, I seem to remember you saying you 'can't bake worth shit' when we first started dating."

"For this, I'm baking, and it won't be shit."

I don't have to be looking at her to know she just rewarded me with a headshake and an eye roll. The stool scrapes against the floor as she moves to stand. "While you're in here throwing around all your vast culinary knowledge, I'm going to get some work done. Should I let Tessa know that bakery she suggested is a no, or . . . ?"

The glare I shoot her only earns a laugh as she walks out of the room and heads to her office. A few months after Tessa moved in with Jase last year, we turned her old bedroom into an office for Winter since she works from home. Well, *we* is a bit misleading since Winter fought me on it the entire time, even after Tessa told her she didn't care if her childhood bedroom remained the same or not. Tessa and Haley had a home with Jase, so Tessa certainly didn't need her room here. And we all—okay, everyone but Winter—agreed it made the most sense to keep Haley's bedroom set up since she spent the night a fair amount, something Tessa never did.

I knew Winter would never do it for herself—would never even *ask* for it—so one day while she was out with the girls, Jase, Adam, and I busted our asses to get the room done for her. Black and white framed photographs of different geographical locations—some she's been to and others we want to go to together someday—hang on soft gray walls. Her desk, a simple black piece with three drawers down one side, sits directly under the window so she can look out over the backyard when she's on a deadline and too pressed to move from her chair.

She was shocked when she got home that night—and, yeah, a little pissed I went behind her back and did it for her even after she insisted she didn't need it. She might not have *needed* it, but after the cramped apartment we shared in Chicago—not to mention the shoebox she lived in all through college—she *deserved* it. Something that was one hundred percent hers.

But the thing she didn't understand—the thing I'm still trying to get her to see—is that this isn't *my* home anymore. It's *ours* and I want her to start treating it as such. That was one tiny step in the right direction. I have my space to do my thing—the kitchen my mom redid shortly before she got sick is any chef's wet dream. And Winter deserved to have something she could feel creative in, especially when she puts her heart and soul into every website design . . . into making sure her business stays afloat. And not just stays afloat, but actually thrives.

Winter's steps echo down the hallway until I can't hear them anymore, and then music floats out of the still-open door. A song I've never heard comes on—she doesn't like to listen to bands she knows while she works because she says she'll be distracted with singing along—and I let it become the background as I finally find my mom's recipe and grab the ingredients I need, fully prepared to make this cake my bitch.

While Winter is lost in her world, I get lost in mine, trying diligently to focus on the recipe so I can replicate it. In the culinary world, it's kind of an unspoken rule that chefs are either fantastic with cooking or baking, but rarely with both. Cooking is where I naturally flourished because there are no rules. Sure, certain flavors marry best with others, but everything is an approximation, a splash of this, a pinch of that. Measuring cups don't factor into my cooking, but they are a necessity in baking. One I don't take to very well.

It's a shitty excuse, but it's the only one I have as Winter and I each take a bite of the vanilla cake with vanilla bean frosting. The texture of the cake is off, crumbly and dry instead of moist and flavorful. The only thing elevating it slightly over the crap we ate earlier today is the frosting I somehow managed to not completely annihilate.

"Mmmm," Winter says, forking another bite from the slice. "This is good."

"It's horseshit."

She laughs around a bite of cake. "It is not. It's good."

"*Good* is not good enough."

Blowing out a breath, she sets the fork down on the

plate, then walks around to my side of the island. Wrapping her arms around my waist from behind me, she rests her head between my shoulder blades, her palms running up and down my abs. "You don't need to take this on, you know."

"Yes, I do." If I'm not here to make sure this area goes off without a hitch, who will be? Jase? He'd eat a pile of literal horseshit as long as it was covered in frosting. I certainly can't help with dresses and I know fuck all about flowers or invitations, so this is the only place I can really contribute to our day.

"No, you don't. Cade." She steps back and turns me around, tucking her fingers into the waistband of my jeans. My cock stirs at her fingers' nearness to it, but I ignore it and focus on Winter. "You don't have to do *everything*. You need to let go of the reins once in a while."

"I—" My retort is cut off by her raised eyebrow.

"It's not just the wedding, either. You're working yourself ragged at the restaurant. You have a sous chef for a reason. You need to let her step up and take the load off you a bit. And the wedding? You've already handpicked the caterer. Honestly, no one is going to notice the fact that the frosting has—gasp!—imitation vanilla extract flavoring in it instead of vanilla beans."

"*I'll* notice," I say like a petulant child not ready to drop an argument he knows he's lost. And I've definitely lost this one, because she's right. The letting go lesson was a hard one to learn, but it's one I had to come to terms with when I left Tessa and Haley behind, and when Winter traveled all over the country. And it's still one I continue to learn every day. It's a difficult habit to break, especially after more than a decade of priding myself on being the one to step up and take responsibility where I could.

"Actually." She stands on her tiptoes and places a kiss on my jaw. Her arms go around my neck and pull me toward her so she can whisper in my ear. "I'm hoping you'll be too busy noticing me to pay attention to much else."

Images flash in my mind—Winter in a long, white dress, her hair pulled away from her face, a smile tugging at her lips as she walks toward me . . . And that's all it takes to ease the tension cloaking my shoulders. The wedding day —the one she's only just recently been able to mention in casual conversation—is coming both faster than I thought possible and slow as fucking molasses. I want her on my arm, by my side as my wife, and I want it now. But more than that, I want her to know that I'm not thinking of anything but her when that day comes. Shitty cake included.

I expel a deep breath, then wrap my arms around her and lift her off her feet as I hug her to my chest. "You're right."

"What's that?" she asks, hand cupped around her ear.

I nip the skin at the side of her palm and say, "You're right. No one else will notice. We can go with"—I swallow down my groan and force the rest of the words out—"Cakes by Mary if that's what you want."

She pulls back and smirks at me, her arms wrapped

around my neck as her feet hover above mine. "Are you kidding? We're not going with her. She doesn't even use real vanilla beans in her vanilla frosting!" The smile she shoots me is blinding, and I couldn't stop myself from kissing her even if I wanted to.

Her mouth opens for me, and I sweep my tongue inside, gripping her ass to lift her higher against me. She holds my face as she tilts her head to deepen the kiss, moaning into my mouth when I reach up and cup a breast in my hand, my thumb running back and forth over the pebbled tip.

Panting, she pulls back and says, "Don't think your kisses are going to distract me from what we're talking about. We'll keep looking until we find someone we both like, okay? But you're not making the cake."

I nod, running my lips up the length of her neck. I'd agree to just about anything right now, especially when she wraps her legs around my waist and grinds down against my cock.

Her breath washes over my ear as she says, "First, though, how about we give Jase a run for his money while we take advantage of this perfectly positioned counter?"

"God, I love you."

We both scramble for each other's clothes, her hands inching up my stomach and chest to rid me of my T-shirt as I pop the button of her jeans, then let her slide down the front of me so I can tug them off. I grip her by the ass and lift her onto the counter at the same time she removes her shirt. My jeans are stalled somewhere around my knees, but I can't be bothered to push them any farther, because Winter's hand is around my cock, guiding me home, and all I care about is the sweet, hot heaven I'm sinking into. I grip her hips and pull her closer to the edge of the counter, thrusting deep at the same time.

"Oh *God*," she moans, her head falling back as her fingernails dig into my ass. "Fast, Cade. Please."

When your woman tells you to fuck her fast, you listen. I slide my hands under her ass, hoping to hold her to me and prevent the counter from digging in with each thrust. She's moaning with abandon as I pump into her, but my balls are already pulling tight, and I can't reach around to give her a helping hand while I'm protecting her perfect little ass.

"Touch yourself, baby. Rub your clit."

Without hesitation, she does as I tell her, sliding her fingers down until they're on either side of my cock as it pistons in and out of her. The unexpected touch has me groaning into her neck, trying to hold back the impending orgasm bearing down on me like a fucking hurricane. I know the second she touches her clit because her back arches, pointing her tits toward my face, and I take advantage, ducking my head to swirl my tongue around one nipple before sucking it into my mouth, hard.

Her breath turns ragged, her nails digging into my skin until finally, she breaks, her pussy squeezing my cock as she comes around me, and that's all it takes to pull me with her. I hold myself as deep as possible as I empty inside her.

"Love you, love you, love you," I say against her sweat-dampened chest.

She runs her hand over my hair, scratching slightly against my head. "I love you, too. But I'm still not letting you make our cake."

I breathe out a laugh against her neck, then press a kiss against her fluttering pulse. "If this is how you plan to distract me from the shitty cake, I'm totally fine with that."

"We did this to beat Jase's record, not to distract you from the cake."

"I hate to tell you this, baby, but we beat Jase's record our first week home. This was totally bonus."

Her cheek puffs against my head in a smile. "That was a fun week."

I hum in agreement, then lift her off the counter and carry her toward the bathroom. "We might not have beat his record in the shower, though. We should probably rectify that."

Her laugh bounces around the walls of the bathroom as I kick the door shut behind us and proceed to forget all about the shitty cake and the mound of responsibilities at the restaurant I need to figure out how to delegate. Everything but the feel of Winter around me and the sound of my name on her lips leaves my brain. At least for now.

FIVE

June 22

winter

I'VE BEEN PUTTING this off for months, and Tessa would kill me if she knew I went dress shopping without her—especially when I keep finding excuses when she asks me to go—but I can't stall anymore. With fifty-nine days— God, only fifty-nine?—until the wedding, I'm still going to have to buy off the rack because there isn't enough time to order a dress in and have it altered. Luckily, this small mom-and-pop bridal salon I've driven by a few times has quite a few dresses to choose from, and they didn't even blink when I told them I didn't have an appointment.

Yeah, *luckily*.

I'm not feeling so lucky now as I'm in a too-small dressing room with billowing dresses boxing me in on all sides. Janet, the sales consultant, looked surprised that I came by myself, but she didn't give me any grief when I said I'd prefer to be in the fitting room alone.

The small, padded bench in the corner calls my name, and I don't hesitate as I fall onto it, staring at yards and yards of silk, organza, and lace. I don't even know what kind of dress I want, because I can honestly say it's nothing I've ever thought of before. When most little girls were busy dreaming up their ideal wedding day, I was scrounging for food and dodging my mother's flavor of the week. And now? After spending the past forty-five minutes strolling through dozens upon dozens of possibilities, to say I'm a little over-whelmed is like saying Lake Michigan is a rain puddle.

This is a day I should've been dreaming about sharing with my mom, and here I am, all by myself because I didn't even want to bother Tessa with it. Truth be told, I didn't want her to witness me having a breakdown and have her think it had something to do with my relationship with Cade, which couldn't be further from the truth. If there's one thing I'm sure of, it's him . . . us.

Just not *me*.

There's no one else in the shop now—most people are probably at work at two thirty in the afternoon on a Wednesday—so the silence in here is almost deafening. At least until my ringtone blares. I fumble into my purse and don't even think before I hit answer, just to get the sound to cease. It's only after the call is connected that I realize it was Tessa's face flashing on my screen.

Squeezing my eyes shut and saying a silent prayer that this is short and sweet, I say, "Hello?"

"Hey, girlie. What's shakin'?"

"Um, not much. Just, um—"

"If you're going to talk about something technical you're doing for a site, don't bother. I don't have any idea what you're saying." Without pausing for my reply, she continues. "Anyway, I set up another appointment for cake testing. Hopefully my brother can force some of these down without grumbling the whole time. I swear, I think we've been to nearly every bakery in Michigan. I know he's a damn good chef, but come *on*, man."

"Yeah, I know," I say, my voice just above a whisper.

"Why are you all quiet?"

"What? I'm—"

"How are the dresses working out for you, honey?" Janet calls through the closed door.

I fumble to mute my phone while I say, "Fine, thanks!" but it's no use. Tessa definitely heard Janet if her gasp is any indication.

"Winter Jacobson. *Are you wedding dress shopping right now?*" She spits the question out like a string of four-letter words.

"Umm . . ." There's no right answer here. If I say no, she'll call me on it, because it's obvious that's exactly what I'm doing. If I say yes, not only will she freak out, but I'll have to try and explain why I didn't tell her I was going in the first place.

"Look, lady," she says in her mom voice, keys jingling in the background. "We're going to officially be sisters in T-minus eight weeks, so you better start acting like it. Now where are you? I have the afternoon off, and Haley's got her art club after school. I can be there in ten to twenty." A door slams, and I imagine she's already in her car, pulling out of her driveway.

Hanging my head, I close my eyes and rattle off the location of the salon before ending the call. Fifteen minutes later, I'm still in the same place, sitting and staring at miles and miles of fabric, when there's a knock at the fitting room door.

"You in there?" Tessa asks.

Without answering, I reach over and unlock the latch so she can come in. Her eyes dart to the dresses hanging on the hooks before they settle on my face, and then her lips turn down in the corners. She squats in front of me, blowing the newly blue streak of hair out of her eyes. "What's up?"

"Just, you know"—I gesture to the dresses—"partici-pating in the second best day in a bride's life."

Her eyebrows climb up her forehead. "God, if this is the second best, I'd hate to see the third. You look like you just kicked a kitten."

I drop my head into my hands and groan. "Sorry. I don't know what's wrong with me."

"I'm going to go out on a limb here and say it's a few things snowballing."

Sighing, I drop my hands and look at her. "Yeah?"

With a nod, she starts ticking off on her fingers. "First, I've never once seen you in a dress, so I imagine you're feeling a bit out of your element. Second, these dresses cost money—a *lot* of money—and you hate spending it on yourself. And third—and I'm guessing this is the biggie—you've got no one here with you." She drops her hand and rests it on her knee. "But more than that, you didn't even think you could call me to come and be here with you."

"No, that's not it at all. I knew if I asked you, you'd come. I just . . ." My shoulders sag as I lean against the hard wall of the fitting room. With a shrug, I say, "I'm a mess, and I knew this would be hard. I didn't want you to have to deal with me and my mommy issues on top of everything you're already doing to help with the wedding."

"Newsflash," she says, jazz hands flying. "I've got mommy issues, too. True, yours was a piece of work and I'm thankful I never had to deal with that, but the bottom line is I don't have a mom to do this with, either. So that means I'm going to count on you to go with me when the time comes and tell me point blank if I can pull off the dress I want or if it makes me look like a walrus. And whether you like it or not, I'm here to do that for you. So it's time to suit up." She moves to stand and plucks the first dress off the hanger, then looks at me with a raised eyebrow, just daring me to challenge her.

Even if I hadn't been around Tessa enough to know

when she's not messing around, the truth is her little speech is exactly what I need. She doesn't sugarcoat things or bullshit her way through any issues, and I appreciate it, even if I *am* out of my element. Being here by myself just showcased so many things I'm already self-conscious about and brought to life memories I'd rather keep buried. Even if it would've been harder to have her here to witness it from the beginning, I should've asked her to come, if for nothing else than to support me when I need it most.

Tessa starts tapping her foot in a silent gesture to hurry the hell up, so I stand and strip down to my bra and underwear, then let her help me into the first of too-many-to-count dresses. And while they're all pretty, and a handful of them fit me perfectly, none of them give me anything resembling butterflies. But maybe I won't get them? With the exception of my feelings for Cade, I'm not exactly a butterflies kind of girl.

"Maybe I should just get this one," I say, tugging out the third dress I tried on. It's all lace with a long train, which is a little over the top for my tastes—not to mention our small, backyard wedding—but it fit me probably the best of all of them, and I liked it okay.

"Not happening." Tessa shakes her head and grabs an armful of dresses to take back out to Janet before inching the door open to sneak out without showing everyone my goodies. "Just sit tight. I'll be right back."

Like I'm going to strut around the store in my underwear.

Tessa's voice carries into the dressing room, along with

Janet's. All kinds of terms I've never once heard of in reference to clothing are mentioned—mermaids and trumpets and chapel trains—and I shift from foot to foot, thumbnail in my mouth as I demolish my cuticle. What seems like a thousand minutes later, there's a knock at the door.

"It's me." Once the door is unlocked, Tessa pokes her head in, dresses still out of view. "Close your eyes and assume the position."

I roll said eyes first, but then comply, arms raised straight in the air while I wait. The door latches behind her, there's some rustling, and then cool, smooth material slides over my skin. It *feels* nice, but then again, most of the ones I've tried—except for the ball gown that weighed at least thirty-five pounds—felt nice.

"Turn around," Tessa says, spinning me by the hips until my back is to her. "And keep your eyes closed!" Then she's hard at work fiddling with something at my lower back, and it takes everything in me not to open my eyes and sneak a glance, especially when she spends nearly ten minutes working on the back of the gown.

"What the hell are you doing back there?"

"Buttons."

"Like . . . real ones?" All the dresses I've tried thus far that had buttons down the back had zipper closures.

"Yes, real ones."

I think about my fiancé trying to get me out of this dress on our wedding night, his large fingers fumbling with what are no doubt minuscule buttons. "Cade's going to hate it."

She laughs as she runs her hands down my sides to smooth the dress and then turns me to face her again. "No, he's not." Her voice sounds suspiciously tight, like she's trying to swallow back tears, but that can't be right. She's been as stone-faced as me this entire time.

"Can I open?"

"Yes, but don't look down. Eyes on me, got it?"

"Sir, yes, sir," I say and open my eyes. And I was right. Hers are glassy, and we'd already agreed there'd be no crying at this party. I jab a finger at her. "I thought I told you no crying."

"I'm not crying. I have an eyelash."

"In both eyes," I say flatly.

She ignores me and unlatches the door to the fitting room, holding it open for me to exit into the main area where they have a pedestal to stand on and a floor-to-ceiling three-way mirror.

"Don't you dare look down before you get to the mirror," Tessa says. "Eyes straight ahead."

"If I trip and rip this dress, you're buying it."

When I get to the pedestal, I reach down without looking and gather up the . . . silk? Satin? And step onto the raised platform, letting the dress drop and lowering my eyes to the mirror in front of me. It takes me a minute to take everything in, from the slim straps to the unobtrusive lace embellishment peeking out of the low, draped neckline to the nearly straight silhouette, flaring just slightly at the bottom where the material pools at my feet. Janet and Tessa stand off to the side, both of them sniffling, but I don't pay attention to them as I twist around and look at the back of the dress. It plunges to just above the small of my back, satin buttons starting there and trailing all the way to the hem.

It's . . .

It's . . .

It's everything I never knew I wanted. Simple, classic, elegant, and sexy with just a touch of femininity.

In a wobbly voice, Tessa says, "She'll take it," and I can't even give her shit for buying my wedding dress when I've yet to say a word. I'm too busy picturing what Cade's face is going to look like when I walk toward him wearing this.

And that's when the dormant butterflies come to life.

SIX

August 6

winter

IT'S fourteen days before our wedding, and I never thought I'd be this calm. It was like a switch flipped that day in the bridal salon after finding The Dress—something I'd assumed would never happen. I figured I'd be walking down the aisle in whatever white dress I could find that fit remotely well. Instead, I'll be walking toward Cade in something that makes me feel . . . amazing.

I never thought a *dress* could have that much of an impact on my emotions, but here we are.

It's the day of our bachelor and bachelorette parties, and Cade and I are watching Haley for a bit while the rest of the group gets things set up—what *things*, I'm not sure, but neither of us mind watching Haley before her babysitter comes to stay the night.

It's nearing a hundred degrees today, which is going to be super fun for the guys and their evening of camping. Haley's in the new pool Jason just installed this year. It's way too fucking big for their yard, but what Haley wants, Haley gets. At least where he's concerned.

Even though I try to avoid it at all costs, I can't help but compare Haley and the little girl I used to be. She's not much younger than I was when my mom left me in that grocery store. It's surreal and bittersweet to see what a six-year-old's life *should* be like, instead of the living nightmare that was my childhood. While Tessa worries Jase spoils Haley, I'm just happy she has someone willing to give her everything she wants—a childhood she can remember with fondness rather than disdain.

"You want another beer, baby?" Cade tips his head in the direction of my nearly finished bottle.

"No, I'm okay. The girls will kill me if I get too much of a head start."

"Have they told you yet where you're going?"

I shake my head. "All I know is I'm supposed to wear whatever Paige left for me. I'm honestly scared to look."

"You should be," he says with a smirk as his eyes rake over me. Nearly a hundred degrees, and my nipples still perk up from his perusal like we're in sub-zero temps.

Before I can ask him what he means by that, Haley pops her head over the side of the aboveground pool. "Hey, guess what?" she yells, like we're not three feet away from her.

"What?" Cade and I ask at the same time. He reaches over and rests his hand on the arm of my chair, running his pinky along the sensitive skin at my wrist. Perked up nipples *and* goosebumps, all from a look and a pinky. He's good.

"We brought my flower girl dress home yesterday! It's hangin' up in my closet. Mama said I couldn't wear it or try it on or even *touch* it, case I had dirty hands. She made me pinky promise."

I smile at her excitement, which hasn't waned at all since the day Tessa, Paige, and I took her to find her dress. Her eyes got so wide when we walked into the store to see aisle after aisle of dresses on display, like a kid in a candy store. I had absolutely no preference about what she wore, so when she said she wanted to look just like a ballerina, that's what she got. I think the skirt of her dress is four times as wide as she is and weighs more than she does.

"I bet you're going to look very pretty," Cade says. "Just like a princess."

"Like a *ballerina*, Uncle Cade." The duh is implied by her tone. She turns her attention to me. "I might even be as pretty as *you*, Aunt Winter!" The smile she shoots me is as bright as the sun beating down on us. Then she pushes away from the side, going underwater as Cade reminds her to be careful. Haley splashes and Cade says something to me, but all the blood is rushing to my ears, my heart beating too fast, my mouth as dry as the Sahara while my world comes to a grinding, screeching halt.

Aunt Winter.

Without blinking an eye or realizing how much it could affect me, Haley made me part of her family with a single word. Part of a family I've been searching my whole life to find.

Whether or not I admitted it to myself, that's exactly what I spent my early years doing. I had the hard exterior to protect myself, but deep down, I wanted to belong. I would've given anything to be taken in. To be *wanted*. But then I decided I didn't need any of it and blocked myself off from everything, building a wall of protection around my heart. A wall Cade managed to knock down with his bare hands.

Since the beginning, he's been trying to show me that his family is my family, but I still feel this divide. Everyone in Cade's life has been nothing but accepting and welcoming, but I'm stubborn and self-sufficient, and I just feel like I'm taking and taking because I don't bring anything to the table. I have nothing else to offer.

It's just me.

And that's never been more apparent than when we were addressing invitations and I had exactly one to fill out for my side. Annette is the one and only person I'm inviting—the one and only person I *have* to invite. And even though it's a small wedding—only a couple dozen guests in total—it's still a blow to realize only one person is coming just for me.

But now . . . with Haley calling me Aunt Winter, it becomes crystal clear it never mattered that I didn't view myself as part of their family. It doesn't matter that I never allowed myself to feel or even *think* that, because everyone else already has been.

And that just makes this all the more real.

This wedding . . . tying Cade to myself for the rest of our lives . . . It isn't just me who could get hurt if all this goes to shit—if I fail at being part of a family. And, really, what the hell do I know about that? The closest thing I had to a normal family life was when I was thirteen and had been placed with a couple for a year. I overheard them talking about taking the steps to adopt me, make me a permanent fixture in their lives. And then after years of trying in vain, they got pregnant and I got shuffled back to the group home I'd managed to escape for a year.

Family has always had a negative connotation in my mind, and that's something that's going to take more than a couple years to erase. It's no doubt why I've resisted putting this amazing group of people into that box that Haley just so casually inserted herself into. It isn't that I don't love them, because I do. Every last one of them.

It's because every single person who I've ever considered family has abandoned me, and maybe if I don't put them in that box, I can keep them a little longer.

I'M NOT sure what drink I'm on. I lost count about twenty minutes after we arrived. What I *do* know is this bachelorette party couldn't have come at a better time. After Haley's declaration this afternoon, I needed some alcohol to quiet the voices in my head and the panic still echoing in my veins. And Paige and Tessa are living up to their bridesmaid duties and getting me full on smashed.

We managed to secure a high top table just off the side of the dance floor. It's packed in here, too many sweaty bodies moving around, but the alcohol thrumming through my body helps to dull it all. Tessa and Paige are both dancing to the beat of the music pounding through the speakers, and I'm clinging to my drink like a lifeline.

Paige leans over the table toward me, shoving a finger in my direction. "Drink up, girl, because we've got more stops!"

"Let's just stay here," I say, lifting my glass, the blue liquid sloshing around as I do so. "Their Adios Motherfuckers are on point."

She slams her hands down on the table, the jolt shaking the liquid in her and Tessa's glasses, a bit spilling over the rims. "We're gonna be saying adios to these motherfuckers in about five minutes. I don't give a shit if they rain money from the ceiling. We're seeing peen tonight, bitches!"

I groan while Tessa just shakes her head. "You know we have three guys who will happily show us their peens, right?" Her words aren't slurred, her response clear, even with the overpowering music.

"Where's the fun in that?" Paige shoots us a sly grin.

Then to me, she says, "Besides, you're kind of mopey tonight, and what better way to get happy than to have junk shaking around in your face?"

I frown and bring the drink to my lips, draining it. Apparently I'm not doing as good a job at hiding as I thought I was. "I'm not mopey..."

"You kind of are," Tessa says with a nod, sipping on her virgin sunrise. She insisted on being DD tonight, and since I planned to get shitfaced, I didn't put up much of a fight. "What's up?"

"What?" I yell, cupping a hand around my ear. "I can't hear you over the music." I wave my hand in a general all-encompassing movement and almost take out a tray of drinks as a waitress walks past. The truth is, I can hear her just fine, but I am definitely not ready to discuss why I feel like my skin is too tight, like I'm trying to claw my way out. Nope, not going there. Not tonight, not ever.

Maybe if I ignore it, it'll go away. That's my motto, and that's what I'm sticking to.

"But seriously," Paige says, "you're mopey, Tessa's not even drinking. What the hell kind of lame-ass bachelorette party is this?"

"I've got a dick on my head, Paige," I say.

"And?"

"And around my neck."

She rolls her eyes. "*And?*"

"Just sayin'. This party's a lot of things, but lame isn't one."

Apparently not satisfied the party isn't lame, she sets

her sights on Tessa, narrowing her eyes. "And *you*. You didn't have to be DD, you know. We could've Ubered."

Tessa shrugs. "I don't mind. Cheaper this way."

"Cheaper . . . who the fuck cares? It's not as fun."

"*I'm* having fun." She pushes the button on her penis tiara, making the erect dick light up in a rainbow of flashing colors. "Whoo! Peen!"

Previously completely drunk Paige suddenly gets sharper, her eyes narrowing on Tessa as she points an accusatory finger in her direction. "Something's not adding up with you."

Honestly, I have no idea what she's talking about, because I just finished my fifth—seventh? Tenth?—drink, and I lost feeling in my face somewhere around drink three. Still, it takes the pressure off me, so I just lean my elbow on the table and bring my straw to my lips, trying in vain to get some more liquid out of the empty glass while I watch the volley between them.

"I have no idea what you're talking about." Tessa looks away and clears her throat. She might as well have shifty eyes for all the anxiety her body language is giving off.

"Mhmm, sure you don't. You've been super distracted lately." Paige slams down her empty glass a little too hard.

"Uh, hello, we're planning a wedding here," Tessa says with an eye roll.

"You've also taken, like, four sick days in the past month. You never do that." Paige's eyes narrow further with every word that comes out of her mouth until she's basically just squinting at Tessa like a pirate. A drunk pirate. *Arrr*. I snort out a laugh, but Paige ignores me as she holds up a hand and ticks off her fingers. "Super distracted, sick all the time, refusing to drink . . . Did you forget I was there the last time?"

I'm still totally lost, but their interaction is too interesting to ignore, so I bounce my eyes between the two of them as they have their verbal match.

"Last time what, Paige? I was sick?"

"Last time you were *sick*? Are you kidding me? Last time you were *pregnant*, slore!" She yells it so loud, several people around us turn to look our way, but she ignores them and focuses on Tessa's face, which has turned fourteen shades of pink. Paige stumbles back, then moves right into Tessa's personal space, their noses inches apart. "Holy shit. It's true, isn't it?"

Tessa glances at me, then at Paige. Blowing out a deep breath, she nods. "I'm sorry, Winter. I wanted to wait until after the wedding to announce it. I didn't want you to feel like I was stealing your thunder."

My thunder? I shake my head because there are words coming out of their mouths, but I have no idea what any of them mean, least of all what they mean strung together like they were. "I don't . . . You're not . . ." I slap my hand on my forehead and put the other one on the table to try and ground myself. This room wasn't spinning a second ago, and now I feel as if I'm on a merry-go-round. "I have no idea what the fuck you're talking 'bout."

Paige grabs me by the shoulders and turns me to face

her, then shakes me hard enough to rattle my teeth. "We're gonna be aunts again! *Huzzah!*" she says with a fist pump.

And just like that, everything I've spent the night blocking out comes rushing back full force, along with the twenty-seven drinks I've downed. "I think . . ." I try to swallow the rush of saliva in my mouth, but it's no use. "I think I'm gonna be sick."

SEVEN

August 6

cade

"JESUS FUCKING CHRIST, it's hotter than the devil's ballsack out here." Jase hefts a cooler filled with enough alcohol to last us a week instead of the single night we're camping. "Whose bright idea was this? It's total bullshit. I want strippers."

I roll my eyes as I lug our tents and a couple backpacks. "I'll be sure to let my sister know that." After two decades of being friends with Jase, I know when he's trying to get a rise out of me, and this is one of those times.

"You're like a goddamn child, you know that?" Adam

passes Jase and manages to shove him, even while carrying the rest of our gear. "We're not hiking three miles, for fuck's sake. You do know we're about forty yards behind the store, right?"

Reid Sporting Goods, Adam's family's store—well, *Adam's* store—sits on the perfect property for a chill night of camping for my bachelor party. The location is within walking distance to a lake for kayaking or canoeing, a hiking trail, and enough climbing opportunities to make even a well-versed climber like Adam happy. We definitely won't be bored, despite Jase's bitching.

Once we reach the place Adam picked out for tonight, Jase sets down the cooler, lifts the lid, and pulls out a bottle of beer without offering one to Adam or me. After closing the lid, he uses it as a seat and pops the cap off his beer before taking a big swallow. "What I know is we should be evening the playing field, is all. Those girls are going to see dick tonight, and it's not going to be ours."

Not taking the bait, I put down the tents and backpacks in the small clearing. "Winter would hate that."

"Unfortunately, that's exactly why Paige would make her go," Adam says, dropping his gear next to mine. He gives me a shrug, like he doesn't care that our girls are going to be inches from some other dude's junk, before knocking Jase off the cooler to pull out beers for both of us.

Well, fuck. Jase blows more smoke out of his ass than a train, but when Adam says it, I listen. And now that he's put it that way, it *is* something Paige would do. With a frown, I grab my phone from my pocket to text Winter, but protests come at me from both sides.

"Put the fucking phone away, Maxwell," Adam says, stern but calm.

Jase just makes some sort of war call and reaches out to hit the phone from my hands. It lands in the grass between me and Adam, who doesn't even blink as he reaches down to pick it up and then pockets it. "You'll get it back when you can start acting like an irresponsible adult."

"Fuck you guys," I say, unloading one of the canvas chairs Adam hauled in and taking a seat.

"Speaking of being a boring middle-aged dude—I mean responsible adult," Jase says, "how're you holding up being here and having fun instead of being stuck at the restaurant tonight?"

"I'm not *stuck* at the restaurant." I shake my head. Neither of them gets it. They both enjoy their jobs, but even Adam, having done a total one-eighty from the accounting job he went to school for to now running the sporting goods store and loving every minute of it, doesn't have the same devotion for what he does as I do. Being a chef isn't just a job to me. It's my *passion*. Even when I'm not at the restaurant, I'm thinking of what new dishes I can create and incorporate into the menu, constantly trying them out on Winter. I live and breathe my profession, and that's never going to change.

"You might not be stuck, man, but you're there all the time," Adam says as he pulls out his own chair and takes a seat.

"So?"

"So . . . you're getting married. You think Winter's going to be okay being the second woman?"

"What the fuck are you talking about? I'd never cheat on her."

Adam tips his bottle in my direction. "But you kind of are. The restaurant might as well be your mistress."

I narrow my eyes at Adam, then glance at Jase, looking for some support from him, but he just shrugs and says, "He's right."

My body goes tight, my shoulders tensing. "Has Winter said something? Did the girls tell you that?"

"Nah, man, I haven't heard anything," Jase says.

Adam confirms the same with a shake of his head. I blow out a breath and relax until he says, "But that doesn't mean she's not thinking it."

These past few months have been a blur, between the wedding planning and work shit. I've been training a new sous chef since the last one got promoted to head chef at another of John's restaurants. I've been putting in a lot of hours there, but that's not anything new.

But maybe that's the problem?

It's never been a secret that I like to be in control of things—hell, it's one of the hardest lessons I had to learn when I first moved to Chicago without Tessa and Haley, and while Winter was traveling all over the country. That need for control extends to my kitchen, too, and Winter knows it. She said as much the first day we went cake tasting. Maybe that was her way of saying she needs more attention from me? That she's not happy anymore?

The beer in my stomach turns to lead as I let that sink in. Jesus, could she just be going through the motions, too scared to say anything about how unhappy she is?

"Fuck," Jase says. "Way to go, Adam, now he's freaking out."

"You're the one who brought it up, asshole." Adam tosses his bottle cap at Jase, who swats it away with a flick of his hand.

"Give me my phone," I say, reaching in Adam's direction.

"Nope," they both say at once.

"Give me my fucking phone. I need to call Winter."

"You sure don't." Jase pulls out his phone and glances at it. "They're coming by later, anyway. Maybe you can use this time to pull yourself together, because you look like a fucking train wreck, man. Pretend like you have a pair of balls in those shorts."

I flip him off, but don't say anything. I can't, really. All I can focus on are the things Winter has said over the past few months. But more than that, it's the things she *hasn't* said. Her hesitant touches, the way she's withdrawn into herself.

Has that all been because of me and my fucking job? Yes, I love it, and I wouldn't be happy doing anything else. Cooking is my passion, but Winter is my *life*. I could take or leave everything else as long as she's by my side.

I just need to make sure she knows it.

ADAM AND JASE tried their hardest to keep my mind off things, forcing us to do everything from hiking to kayaking, but nothing helped. Even when Jase tried to distract me with tales of what he planned to do to my sister tonight, I wasn't bothered. I was too focused on Winter. When that didn't pull a reaction out of me, Adam declared it a lost cause and led us back to the camping site, then proceeded to ply me with alcohol.

Finally, after what seems like a week, I hear a car pull up, followed by loud and unmistakably drunk voices. I don't wait to see if Adam and Jase are following me before I'm out of my chair and walking up the hill toward the parking lot.

"Sounds like we should've pulled out the hard stuff instead of the beer," Jase says behind me. "They're about five rounds ahead of us."

"Fine by me," Adam says. "I'm damn glad for those five extra rounds, because that means Paige is going to rip my pants off in about three minutes."

Before Jase can say anything about Tessa doing the same to him, I speed up to get to Winter faster. I need to see her . . . talk to her. Ask her if she's feeling what I fear she is—that she's second place in my life—and I don't want to wait until tomorrow. I don't want to wait another *minute*. Hopefully she isn't as drunk as the commotion indicates. But when the car comes into view in the parking lot, and three girls stumble out of it—or two very drunk girls and one sober Tessa trying to corral them—that hope is dashed.

"Can you guys come get your women?" Tessa tries to support Winter while holding Paige back by the material of her shirt, but she breaks free and is halfway to us before Tessa can blink.

"Looks like someone had fun," Adam says as he goes straight to Paige. "You feeling okay, cuddle lump?"

Paige throws her head back and laughs, then falls into Adam and whispers something to him. Except it's not a whisper at all, and I cringe, scrubbing a hand over my face. I definitely could've done without hearing what she plans to do in their tent tonight. Before Paige can say anything else totally inappropriate, Adam lifts her into a fireman's carry and hauls her off just as I get to Winter. She's slumped against Tessa's side, her eyelids droopy, but a smile sweeps over her face when she sees me. That's good, right?

"Hey, baby," I say, wrapping my arm around her and letting her lean against me.

"You're so pretty," she says—or slurs, anyway—as she reaches up and pets my face.

I glance at Tessa with eyebrows raised. "How many drinks did you let her have?"

"*Let* her? Have you met your fiancée? I tried to cut her off at five, but she kept sneaking off to the bar and ordering more." She leans into Jase's side as he presses a kiss to her head. Her features are pinched, and that only makes me worry more. Did Winter say something to her and Paige while they were out?

"What is it?" I ask.

Before she can answer, Winter slumps farther into me, her legs nearly giving out. Without thinking twice, I slip my arm under her knees and lift her to my chest. She sighs against my neck and presses a kiss there as she wraps her arms tighter around me.

"Tess?" I ask again.

She glances at Jase, then Winter, whose eyes are now closed. "She got kind of upset tonight. I think it started earlier when you guys were watching Haley and then tonight . . ." She looks over at Jase, then reaches for his hand before looking back at me. "I'm not sure how much she'll remember, but we should talk in the morning."

Fuck. My heart free falls to my stomach, and I can't seem to swallow the gravel stuck in my throat. I manage a nod and turn, bringing Winter toward our tent while Jase and Tessa follow before veering off for theirs. Squeals and laughter come from Adam and Paige's tent, but I block them out as I get Winter inside ours.

Once we're zipped up in our small, two-person tent, I set her down on the sleeping bag I laid out earlier. She flops back with a sigh, wiggling to get comfortable. I slip her shoes from her feet, rubbing my thumbs into her arches. She moans, pushing her feet farther into my hands, but doesn't say anything. The dress Paige laid out for Winter earlier is even more minuscule now that it's on her body, the hem creeping up far enough to reveal her panties. I go to my bag and rummage around until I find one of my T-shirts.

"Baby," I say, leaning over her and brushing the hair back from her face. "You want to change into this?"

Her eyelids flutter open and she sits up, hands straight in the air. With a chuckle, I help her out of her dress before slipping my shirt over her head. Once she's covered, she lies back down, gripping the front of my shirt to pull me with her. As I lie down at her side, she snuggles into me, pressing her nose into my neck, her leg thrown over mine.

"Missed you," she says through a yawn.

She's awake, but not by much. She's going to pass out any second, so I don't want to get to the crux of what I need to know only to have her fall asleep mid-convo. Instead, I ask, "Did you have fun?"

"Mhmm . . . till Tessa broke my thunder," she mumbles.

Broke her thunder? What the fuck does that mean? "What'd Tess do?"

Silence greets me, and I glance down. Winter's eyes are closed, deep breaths passing through parted lips. Her arm is heavy against my chest, telling me she's well and truly out for the night. Meanwhile, I'm rigid as hell, a hundred possibilities flying through my head at what Tessa's—and now Winter's—comments mean. Ten minutes later, I can't take it anymore and slip out from under Winter, heading straight for Jase and Tess's tent. It's quiet, just some unintelligible murmurs drifting out. No moans, thank Christ.

"You two better be dressed, because I need to talk."

"*Knew* that sad bastard wouldn't let me get lucky tonight," Jase mumbles as Tessa laughs. She undoes the zipper and then steps out, Jase behind her.

"We took bets on how long it'd take you to come over here." Tessa leans back into Jase's chest as he wraps an arm around her shoulders from behind. "I won, by the way. I think Jase was optimistic."

"I knew you'd be over here this soon, too, but my 'loss' isn't exactly a hardship, if you know what I mean," Jase says, wiggling his fucking eyebrows.

I take a deep breath, rubbing my finger and thumb against my eyes, not even bothering to snap at him for that comment. "I just need to know what's bothering Winter. Was she upset all night?"

Tessa blows out a deep breath. "Well, no, not exactly, but she wasn't herself. She didn't want to talk much until she got a few drinks in her, then she kept telling us she just wanted to keep us a while longer. I have no idea what she meant, but thought you might?"

Keep them a while longer? I shake my head. "No idea. She also said you broke her thunder. No clue what she's talking about there either."

Tessa stiffens, her fingers white-knuckling Jase's forearm, and he presses a kiss to her temple. "Just tell him, baby," Jase says. "It's okay."

I divide my attention between the two of them, narrowing my eyes. "Tell me what?"

"I didn't break her thunder," Tessa says. "I was worried

about *stealing* her thunder. We wanted to wait until after the wedding to tell everyone."

Stealing her thunder . . . waiting until after the wedding . . . ? I shoot my eyes to Tessa's left hand, which is still clutching Jase's arm. No ring, but that doesn't necessarily mean anything. And even though Jase didn't ask me to go ring shopping, I wouldn't put it past the bastard not to ask me as payback for finding Winter's ring on my own. "Did Jase propose?"

"Not yet," Jase says, and there's the tiniest bit of challenge in his voice, like he's expecting me to fight him on it.

"Then what . . . ?"

But then I notice his hand spread out almost protectively across Tessa's abdomen at the same time she says, "You're gonna be an uncle again."

"Holy shit," I say. Then louder, "Holy *shit*." For the briefest moments, my concern over Winter recedes as I bring Tessa into a hug before doing the same for Jase. While I'd rather not think about my best friend knocking up my sister, I can't deny that he treats both her and Haley like princesses. He'd do anything for them, and I know it'll be the same with the baby. I can't ask for anything more for my baby sister and niece, despite all the grief I gave Jase and Tess when they first got together.

"When's the baby due?" I ask.

"February twentieth," Tessa says, leaning once again into Jase, her eyes studying mine. "You're not mad?"

"Why the hell would I be mad about getting another niece or a nephew?"

She shrugs. "I don't know . . . We're not married. I've been here before."

"You have *not* been here before, Tess. Totally different circumstances."

"Well, yeah, I know that, but . . ."

"You thought I wouldn't see it like that?" I shake my head and tell her honestly, "If I had to pick someone for you to have more babies with, it'd be Jase. Married or not. I'm happy for you guys."

"Thank you," Tessa says, her shoulders visibly relaxing.

"Happy for you, but I'm still going crazy over here. I need to know what the hell happened with Winter tonight."

"Right . . ." Tessa nods, tucking her hair behind her ear. "So she kept talking about not wanting us to be family so she could keep us. I have no idea what it means, and after I told her about the baby, it only got worse. She just kept repeating that she didn't want to be an aunt because she wanted to keep us a little longer." She shakes her head. "I thought it might mean something to you."

Whether or not she wants to be an aunt is irrelevant, because Haley loves her to death. She's been Aunt Winter for months and months, but today was the first time Haley's ever said it directly to Winter. I wonder if that's where it stemmed from? It doesn't take a genius to figure out she doesn't have the best outlook when it comes to family. And despite attempting to show her otherwise, that our family means something different, I've been leaving her to fend for herself while I focused on the restaurant.

That ends right now. I still have responsibilities there and always will. But I can take some time and show Winter exactly what being part of my family means, reassure her she's the most important thing in my life. And that won't change, no matter how much she fears it's going to.

EIGHT

August 13

cade

THIS HAS BEEN the longest goddamn week of my life, but I needed to get things in order at work, and make sure my sous chef, Kat, was confident running the restaurant on the busiest day of the week. If I plan to change how much time I'm spending at the restaurant, I need to get used to this. I don't want to work every weekend for the rest of my life. Before this month, with the bachelor party, wedding, and now the little getaway I planned that Winter and I are currently en route to, I can count on one hand how many weekends I'd had off since I became head chef. That shit's about to change. I'll still have to work many—I *want* to, because there's nothing quite like the rush of a good dinner service, and it's almost guaranteed on a Saturday night—but I don't have to work them all.

Winter's hand is encased in mine over the center console, her lips moving along with the song playing on the radio. She's been quiet since last weekend, more so than usual, and it's killed me not to talk to her about it. The morning following the bachelor and bachelorette parties only reaffirmed my need to show her what it means to be part of my family. And let her know that whether or not she includes herself in that group, she's in it. God, the thought that she didn't put herself there about killed me. Before we packed up to leave, the six of us were sitting around in the circle created by our chairs when Baby Maxwell-Montgomery was brought up. As the rest of us talked about details—due dates and when they were going to tell Haley and if they were going to find out if it was a boy or a girl—Winter sat in my lap, stiff as a board, and no amount of back rubbing calmed her. No amount of reassurance on my part did anything to help her relax. And, as far as I can tell, those nerves haven't abated at all in the past week. If anything, they've increased, no doubt because of the upcoming wedding.

"We're sure driving far for dinner," she says, glancing out the window.

I shrug. "John mentioned this place, and I want to check it out." All true, fortunately. *This place* just refers to a bed and breakfast instead of a restaurant like she assumes.

Unsure what she'd need for the weekend, I filled a bag with everything of hers from the bathroom, then threw in a few different pieces of clothing. If I have it my way, we'll spend most of the time naked and in bed, anyway, so she won't need clothes at all.

"I can't believe you got another Saturday off." She looks over at me. "Are you sure that's okay? That'll be three in a row with the wedding next weekend . . ."

"John understands and trusts my decisions for the restaurant." I squeeze her hand and glance at her before returning my attention to the road. "Like you said, I hired a sous chef for a reason."

I feel her eyes on me, but she just hums in response, and she doesn't say anything the rest of the drive. When we finally get to the small town a little less than an hour from home, her brow is furrowed as she looks out the window, no doubt trying to figure out where we are. When I pull into the parking lot of the bed and breakfast, she turns to me with narrowed eyes.

"Do they have a restaurant in here?"

"Not exactly." I shut off the car, then get out before going over to her side and opening her door. Reaching for her hand, I help her out, then go to the trunk and grab our bags while she stands off to the side, mouth agape.

"Cade Brendon Maxwell, what did you do?"

"C'mon and you'll find out." I smile and tug her along behind me.

After checking in at the front desk, we're shown to our room, complete with outside entrance, private bath, and fireplace. John outdid himself with this recommendation. Once inside our room, I drop our bags on the bed and turn to find Winter staring at me, arms crossed against her chest.

"What is all this, Cade?"

I walk over to her and tug her to me, pressing a kiss on her neck. "It's me showing you how much I love you."

Where she was stiff just a moment ago, she relaxes at my words, her arms going around my waist as she sighs. "You don't need to bring me to a bed and breakfast an hour away to show me that. I already know it."

"Do you?"

"Of course," she says, stepping back, the irritation written plainly on her face. "What the hell kind of question is that?"

"The guys were talking—"

She groans. "For the record, I hate when you start stories like that, because they generally don't end well. And your best friends . . . They're great, but they can be idiots."

"I'm definitely not arguing that, but what they said this time got me thinking. And worrying . . ."

If I wasn't paying close attention, I would've missed how her shoulders stiffen again as soon as the words are out of my mouth. Even with her tense body language, her voice is casual as she asks, "About what?"

I sit at the foot of the bed, then reach for her hand and guide her to stand between my knees. With my hands resting on her hips, I look up at her. "I need you to be honest with me, baby. Okay?"

Her throat bobs as she swallows, her eyes darting between mine. With a nod, she says, "Okay."

I run my thumbs on the soft skin of her stomach, just above her waistband. "Do you feel like you're second place?"

She's frozen for about five seconds before confusion sweeps over her face. Her brow furrows, the corners of her mouth curving down in a frown. "Second place to what?"

"The restaurant."

"What?" She jerks back, already shaking her head. "No, Cade. I've never felt like that."

"Because it would be understandable, especially since I've been so focused on it."

"Of course you have. You've been getting it up and running. We knew that going in."

I nod, recalling the discussion we had back in Chicago, talking about what kind of sacrifices we'd have to make if we made the move, if I accepted the job. We both agreed to them, but . . . "Things change."

"They do, but not with this. I don't mind that you're working so much. I *love* that you're able to do what you love for a living."

Hearing her say that lifts a huge weight from my shoulders, and I sag with relief, dropping my forehead to her stomach. She brings her hands to my hair and rubs in soothing strokes. It's almost enough to make me fall back on the bed and pull her with me, then focus on getting her naked and under me, but I can't get her words from last weekend out of my head. I've tried to puzzle them out over the past week, and I just can't get them to make sense.

Pulling back, I look up at her. Her hair falls around her shoulders, the fresh scent of her shampoo surrounding me. She's got a soft smile on her lips as she stares at me, and she's so fucking beautiful it hurts. And in a week, she's going to be my wife.

"Last weekend, you kept saying you wanted to keep us a while longer." Squeezing her hips, I ask, "What did you mean?"

Her caressing hands freeze against the back of my neck, her body stiff under my hands. She parts her lips, then closes them again, shaking her head. "I . . . I don't know."

I raise an eyebrow. "You said you'd be honest with me. After two years, I can tell when you're lying."

She exhales a deep breath, her shoulders slumping as she does so. "It's not a big deal."

"If it's been upsetting you, it *is* a big deal. And you should've talked to me about it. You promised me you wouldn't push me away anymore, and keeping this to yourself is the same thing. I want to know what's been bothering you." I pull her a little closer. "Time's up, baby."

She pulls her lip between her teeth and bites down hard enough that I cringe. I grip the backs of her thighs and tug her up into my lap, her knees resting on either side of my hips. Her hands still have a death grip on the back of my neck, and while normally her body would melt into mine in this position, it's rigid, the line of her back straight and her thighs bunched tight under my roaming hands.

When she doesn't say anything after a several long moments, I ask, "Winter, do you still want to marry me?" It kills me to ask it, mostly because I'm scared shitless about what the answer might be, but if we're going to work through whatever issues we've got, one of us has to ask the tough questions, and it's sure as hell not going to be bury-her-head-in-the-sand Winter.

She stares at me, darting her gaze between my eyes, and gives a nod. "Yes."

I don't even realize how much tension I was holding in my shoulders until her answer causes me to blow out a relieved breath, my entire body relaxing as I do so. "Glad we're on the same page there." I smile, giving her a soft kiss. "So you want to marry me, and you've spent the past several months trying to figure out how to be a better partner . . . a better wife, right?" The words are ridiculous —were ridiculous when she told me the first time, and feel even more ridiculous coming out of my mouth. If I wasn't completely happy with Winter as she is, why the hell would I have proposed in the first place? I still don't understand why she hasn't gotten that yet.

She gives me another slow nod, but this time, her forehead's creased, like she's trying to figure out where I'm going with this.

"Well, here's the thing. There's some crazy talk going around that open, honest communication is the key to a successful marriage." I hook my fingers in her back belt loops and rub my thumbs along the small of her back. "So you can bring me all the extra candy you want—don't think I haven't noticed that, by the way—and I can take you to surprise weekend getaways, but if we don't have the basics down . . . Baby, we're doomed. I need you to talk to me. Can you do that?"

I can see the minute she realizes I'm right. That she has to do this if she wants our relationship to survive the next fifty years. And she does see it—that much is clear as I watch her expression change. How she goes from scared to resigned to determined.

Finally, she nods. "You're right. I know you are. And I want to talk to you, I do. But"—she glances down, watching the movement of her hand as she trails it down my chest to rest over my heart—"can you give me a little time alone? Just to get my thoughts in order?"

If a while by herself is what she needs to work up the courage to talk to me about whatever has been bothering her, I'll give it to her. Honestly, I'd give her a lifetime if it made it easier for her. "Sure, baby, whatever you need. How about I go find something for dinner?"

She blows out a breath, her body finally relaxing as she wraps her arms around me in a hug. "Thank you." Her voice is quiet next to my ear, just the barest of whispers, but I hear it all the same.

If I thought the past week was long, I'm willing to bet it's going to have nothing on how long the next couple hours will feel.

winter

CADE'S BEEN GONE for over an hour, but this panic bubbling into my throat hasn't lessened at all. With two words, he succinctly summed up exactly what I've been feeling for the past several weeks. *Time's up.* But how do I tell him that? How do I share with him fears that don't even make sense to me? Fears I know are unfounded, but are there all the same, weighing me down, tainting everything. It's like all the stress of a wedding multiplied by a thousand, because one thought plays over and over in my mind, like a broken record.

What if I'm not enough to keep him?

I have no family, all but one of the friends I'm lucky enough to have in my life have come from him, and I have no fucking idea how to give him the kind of life he deserves —the kind of *family* he deserves.

If I can't keep him, not only would I lose him—the only person who's ever loved me for me—but I'd lose the people I've come to consider family, despite how badly I've tried to avoid it.

There's only so much heartbreak a person should be expected to suffer in a lifetime. I'm just not sure I could survive the aftermath of being left again.

Even having this all worked out in my head, I have no idea how to go about actually sharing it with Cade, despite the fact that I know he's right. If I want our marriage to survive, I need to be able to be honest with him about this —about *everything*. The kicker, though, is that I don't even know what he could possibly do to actually help. It's not as if he doesn't show me he loves me. His fear that I would feel like I was second place to his career couldn't be further from the truth. It's actually a bit of a relief to know he has certain doubts, too, but that he'd doubt for a minute that I see his love every day in the little—and big—things he does for me is crazy.

And that's the thing . . . if he already shows me that, if I already feel his love, what will it take to finally get through to me and put these fears to rest once and for all?

I'm not any closer to an answer when he walks through the door much later. He's been gone for almost three hours, but it might as well have been three minutes for all the good the time alone has done me.

"Hey, baby," he says as he steps through the door, locking it behind him. He comes over to where I'm perched at the foot of the bed and leans down to give me a kiss, pressing his lips to mine. "I hope you're hungry. I got enough Thai to feed an army."

I relax slightly, though I'm not sure why I thought he'd walk through the door and demand I start talking immediately. He's not like that—has never been like that. He'll let me do this on my time, if that's what makes me comfortable. I follow him to the small dining table in the corner to help him unload. He's already pulling boxes out of the bag, working quickly as he gets everything laid out for us.

As he places a carton close to me, writing on his left

hand catches my eye. I don't think as I reach out and grasp his hand in mine, tugging it to me for a closer look. For a split second, I think it's marker. It has to be. Because even though that'd be a little weird—that he randomly scrawled my name on his finger—it's easier to process than the alternative. But then I notice the slight sheen on the base of his finger—exactly what Cade's skin looks like after he's gotten a fresh tattoo—and I realize the single word on his left ring finger isn't in his handwriting . . . It's in mine.

Winter.

Right there, for all the world to see, a week before our wedding is even supposed to take place, he's branded himself with my name. Thoughts come rushing back to me of the night years ago, when Cade followed me onto the bus after he was a no-show at our unspoken date the previous two evenings. How he sat across from me, begging me for a date. How disappointed I was when I saw Haley's name on his arm, assuming it was his girlfriend, and wondering what it'd be like to be loved by someone so much they'd want to mark themselves forever with your name.

I don't have to wonder anymore.

"Cade. Oh my God. *Cade.*" My heart's beating too fast, and I don't know whether to puke or scream. "Holy shit. Holy *fuck*. You can't—what if you . . ." I stumble through my thoughts, until suddenly they rush out of me like a tsunami. "God, what if you figure out I'm not enough? That I don't have anything to offer you! I had one measly person to invite to the wedding. I don't have anyone else!

And then—*shit*—I was stressing about being an aunt to one kid and now I have to take on *two*. And what if *we* have kids? Oh my God. If I'm freaking out about kids who aren't even mine, *what then?* You can't just leave the tattoo behind like you can me! Why would you do that? Why would you *do* that?"

He ducks to try and catch my eye, but I can't take mine off his newly marked skin. "This is all because you're worried about not having anyone at the wedding?" he asks, his voice somehow calm while my throat is raw from yelling. "Baby, I don't care if we go to the Justice of the Peace right now and get married with people they had to pull in as witnesses. If it ends with you as my wife, I'm happy. That's all I care about."

I scoff, pulling away as I pace the room, digging the heels of my hands against my eyes. My skin's getting too tight, invisible fingers creeping up my neck and closing around my throat, and I can't breathe. "It's more than not having anyone to invite to the wedding, Cade! It's about not being able to give you the family you deserve."

"Baby," he says, stopping my pacing and pulling me into his lap. He brushes the hair back from my face. "Breathe. Winter, you need to breathe."

It's only then that I realize I'm damn close to hyperventilating, my body covered in a light sheen of sweat. And suddenly I can't hold back the tears. It's all too much. Everything I've been feeling since I woke up with his ring on my finger comes pouring out of me. All I manage to get out is one word, over and over again.

Why. Why? *Why?*

Cade holds me to him, his left hand trapped between us as I clutch it to my chest. He presses kisses anywhere he can reach while his right hand rubs circles against my back, and he answers every one of my *why*s with, "Because I love you."

When my throat is sore and my eyes are puffy and itchy, I'm finally cried out. He sits silently for a few minutes, his calm comforting in the face of my panic. Eventually, he shifts enough to pull something from his pocket, then slides it into my hand. Through swollen eyes, I glance down at the multi-folded postcard.

"Open it," he says, pressing a kiss to my temple.

Not wanting to release my hold on his hand, I fumble with the paper one-handed. To anyone else, it'd look like a generic postcard—just a picture of the Seattle Space Needle. But not to me. I recognize this postcard, and even before I flip it over, I know the exact words that will be written there.

No matter where I am, you're my home.

And then I signed my name, never guessing that a year later, he'd use the same six letters to brand himself forever.

"I remember the day I got that in the mail," he says against my temple. "You'd already left Seattle and were headed to New Mexico by the time it showed up in Chicago. I missed you so fucking much while you were gone, but I wanted you to do what you needed to. And I wanted you to do it without having my issues weighing you down, but I was scared, baby. I was so fucking scared you wouldn't come back to me." He hugs me closer to him, burying his nose into my neck and breathing me in. After a moment, he says, "And then I got this in the mail, and it was like everything clicked. I wasn't scared anymore, because I knew it was the same for you as it was for me. I've carried it around in my wallet ever since to remind me."

He pulls back far enough to meet my eyes, wrapping his fingers around the back of my neck as his thumb caresses my jaw. "I'm going to say this to you, and I want you to listen to me, okay?" He waits for my nod, then says, "*You* are the family I deserve. I don't know what I did to make you think this thing between us was optional for me. That I didn't need you to fucking *breathe*." He brings my left hand to his lips, kissing my engagement ring. "You think even without this tattoo on my finger, you haven't marked me forever? Whether it's your literal name on me or not, I'm *yours*, Winter. I always have been, and this is me trying to show you that's not going to change. You don't have to be worried I'm going to bail or get fed up or tired of you. I'm in this with you, baby. For the rest of our lives."

Somehow, though I thought I cried myself out, a few tears manage to slip down my cheeks again at his words. Cade leans forward and kisses them all away, whispering all the while how much he loves me. How much he needs me. How he can't live without me.

It's everything I've waited my whole life to hear. Everything I've spent most of my years secretly dreaming of, even though I lied to myself about it and did whatever I could to avoid it.

Maybe it's that it's happening *now*, at this exact moment in time, or maybe it's because he took these specific steps to show me how much I mean to him. Or maybe it's because he shared an insecurity he felt. I don't know what it is, but instead of hearing him through the filter I erected long ago, picking and choosing what words got through, I let every single one of them seep in. Let them settle into my bones until I feel them so deep inside me, I'm not sure where they end and I begin.

I don't know how I got lucky enough to call this man mine, but I did. Somehow, despite my childhood and all the baggage that comes along with it, I did. And I'm done questioning it. I'm done living my life perched on the cliff of a bunch of *what if*s. I'm ready to start the rest of our lives together, right now. No fear. No questioning. No uncertainty.

Just love.

NINE

August 20

winter

I THOUGHT I'd be a panicked mess. Assumed I'd be breathing into a paper bag or chewing my nails to the quick, but I'm not. I can't believe that's how this day is playing out, but I don't feel even an ounce of nerves. Instead, I'm . . . excited. And anxious. Not in a bad way, but in a let's-hurry-up-and-get-to-the-good-stuff way. I can't wait to see Cade, can't wait to see the look on his face when he sees me in my dress, can't wait for him to become my husband.

Unfortunately, the nerves that aren't present in me have completely taken over Tessa. She flits about, making sure everyone's hairstyles are staying exactly how she wants them, even though I'm pretty sure the fourteen cans of hairspray she used will do the trick. Hair was something I let her have free rein over, obviously. I wasn't going to tell the hair stylist thanks but no thanks.

And actually, I let her have free rein over most things, because those items just weren't important to me. The hairstyles (mine down and loosely curled—just how Cade likes it, she said), bridesmaid dresses (short, strapless, and navy blue), and flowers (sunflowers, white roses, and daisies), were all her suggestions, and I just went along with it.

Turns out the only thing I really care about is exactly what Cade told me last weekend. As long as the day ends with me being his wife, I'm happy.

"Holy shit, we've only got five minutes," Tessa says, fussing with another piece of my hair. "Paige!"

"I'm right here, Captain Crazypants," Paige says from the couch, flipping through a magazine. "Honestly, this isn't Kate and Prince William's wedding. You can chill the fudge sticks out."

"What's that mean, Auntie Paige?" Haley asks from her spot next to Paige, mimicking her as she turns the pages in her own magazine.

"It means your mom is going cuckoo," she says, making a silly face at Haley, who dissolves in a fit of giggles.

Tessa shoots Paige a glare, then turns back to me, adjusting my hair once more and smoothing the nonexistent wrinkles in my dress. "I just want everything to be perfect for you," she says to me.

"Is Cade standing out there?" I ask.

She freezes in what she's doing and meets my eyes, then steps off to the side and looks out the window into her childhood backyard. I haven't even seen how they set it up —more of Tessa's doing—and while I'm excited to see it, as long as Cade is standing at the end of the aisle, I'll be happy.

When she turns back to me, she nods, smiling, but her eyes are shiny with tears.

"Seriously? Are you *crying* because your brother—*the groom*—is standing exactly where he's supposed to be standing?" Paige asks.

"Shut up," Tessa says, dabbing at her eyes. "I can't wait to see what you're like when you're walking around with all these crazy hormones." She waves a hand in the general vicinity of her nearly unnoticeable baby bump, hidden under the flowing fabric of her dress.

"Gonna have to wait a while for that." Paige stands and tosses her magazine onto the couch, then plucks Haley's from her hand before picking up her bouquet. "Showtime, Haley girl. Grab your basket. Let's get this show on the road."

THE GUESTS ARE ALL SITTING, their eyes focused on Tessa and Jason, then Paige and Adam walking down the aisle, followed immediately by Haley as she tosses flower petals down. As I step out from the side of the house, I can make out enough of the back yard to see Tessa did an amazing job decorating for our small wedding, keeping it low key and simple while making it absolutely breathtaking.

The music changes, the notes signaling my entrance, and I take a deep breath. Two dozen guests move to stand in front of white wood folding chairs, set up on either side of a flower petal-strewn aisle. Strings of lights are hung above them, anchored on either side by the massive trees in our backyard, and dozens of small glass bottles filled with sunflowers and daisies hang from the branches.

The walk to the aisle from the side of the house is the longest seventeen steps of my life. And then I'm there and Cade's waiting for me at the end and I can't take my eyes off him. The gray suit fits him impeccably, his broad shoulders filling out the jacket to a distracting degree. I can count on one hand the number of times I've seen him dressed up, and while I definitely prefer his casual clothes for every day, I can't deny how hot he looks like this, with just the barest hints of his tattoos peeking out of the collar and cuffs of his tailored dress shirt. His lips part as he looks his fill of me, his gaze sliding down the length of my body encased in white silk before he meets my eyes, and then his lips lift in a smile. It's a smile that takes my breath away— one that says I'm his whole world. I can't break away from his gaze for a second, even to look at the guests who showed up for our special day.

He's all I see.

Instead of waiting for me at the end of the aisle like he's supposed to, he steps toward me until suddenly he's right in front of me, and then his hands are cupping my face, his eyes staring down at me.

"You are beautiful," he says just before he presses his lips against mine. The kiss is soft and sweet, the hoots, laughter, and clapping of our guests fading into the background as Cade cradles my face like I'm the most precious thing in the world to him and kisses me over and over again.

"Hey, lovebirds!" Paige says. "The quicker you guys get up here and let this nice man perform the ceremony, the faster you can sneak off and do more of that."

Another wave of laughter echoes around us as Cade and I break apart with a smile, then he links my arm through his and walks me the rest of the way down the aisle.

With his eyes never straying from mine, he tells the officiant, "Get this done as fast as humanly possible, please. I'm ready for her to be my wife."

Funny thing . . . I'm finally ready for that, too.

cade

THOSE WERE the longest hours of my life, being able to touch Winter but not being nearly close enough. It's well after midnight by the time we're finally alone, and I'm seconds away from being inside her.

Or I would be if I could figure out how to get my wife out of this damn dress.

My wife.

Jesus, I'm not sure I'll ever get used to that, but if the past several hours are any indication, I'm going to say and think it as much as possible just to test the theory.

"How many fucking buttons are on this thing?" I ask as I fumble with her dress.

"I told Tessa you'd hate the dress," Winter says, laughter in her eyes as she looks at me over her shoulder.

"I don't hate it. I *love* it." And I do. Whenever I pictured Winter walking down the aisle toward me, I never had a clear idea of what kind of dress she'd be in, but the one she picked—the one that shows off all her curves, that hugs her body and makes her look like a fucking goddess— is perfection.

Moving her hair out of my way, I kiss down her back until I'm on my knees behind her, trying to get my overgrown fingers to work with these toddler-sized buttons. She's no doubt exhausted after the day she's had—hell, I am, too. That's one thing people don't mention when talking about the wedding night. Honestly, I'd be happy just to have her fall asleep in my arms and wake up with her next to me. But if I can do all that after being inside my wife, all the better.

"You want me to help you?" she asks.

"No." I press a kiss to the indentation of her spine, just above the small of her back. "I'll get it."

She shudders, goosebumps covering the skin I can see. Reaching back, she tugs me closer to her and says, "Well, hurry up. I'm impatient to fuck my husband."

Jesus Christ.

Apparently all I needed was a little incentive, because I get the buttons undone and the dress off in four minutes flat. And then she's standing there in front of me in the tiniest pieces of white lace lingerie I've ever seen. I think my cock might actually find a way to escape the confines of my dress pants without any help.

Especially when she steps toward me, her breasts directly at eye level. Her nipples are hard, already straining under the sheer lace. Leaning forward, I suck one into my mouth through the material as I try to get out of this suit as quickly as possible. Winter's moans only spur me on faster, especially when she brings one hand to the back of my head and holds me to her while the other delves into the front of her panties. I've managed to rid myself of everything but my pants and boxers, but I can't wait anymore.

I grip her under her ass as I stand, carrying her toward the bed. "You did that on purpose," I say as I toss her onto the bed, then cage her in under me.

"Did what on purpose?" she asks, looking at me with a glint in her eyes.

And, Christ, I never thought I'd be so happy to see a teasing expression on her face, but the relief is palpable. All day, throughout the ceremony and then the reception, I watched her. Looking for signs of nerves. Of uncertainty or regret. And all I saw was happiness radiating out of her.

Lowering my head, I nip at her bottom lip. "You know exactly what you did, Mrs. Maxwell." I suck her lip into my mouth, then let it go with a pop. "Your husband wants to be the one who gets this pussy worked up, so stop playing with it."

She breathes out a laugh as I make my way down her body, until my shoulders are parting her thighs and I'm hovering right over exactly where I want to be. Her laugh turns into a breathless moan as I lick her through the lace of her panties, pulsing my tongue right against her clit.

"Cade," she says, all breathless and wanting, and the sound manages to harden my cock even further.

Normally, I'd work her up—tongue her pussy until she comes against my mouth, until she's begging me to fuck her —but the honest truth is I can't wait tonight. I can't wait another minute to find out what it feels like to be inside my wife.

After shoving the pants and boxers from my legs, I strip her until she's bare under me, and then I'm rocking into her, sliding into all that perfection.

"*Jesus*." I grasp her hip with one hand and slip my other underneath her back to grip her neck, balancing my weight on my forearm. Rolling my hips, soft and slow, I stare down at her. Her breath is coming out in pants as she digs her fingers into the flesh of my shoulders, my arms, my ass.

"Cade," she breathes. "Faster, please."

I'd normally respond to that request on her lips by snapping my hips forward. But not tonight. Tonight, I want slow. Tonight, I want to take in every tiny detail so I can remember it forever. How her lips part as she pants my name. The feel of her breath against my face. The look in her eyes as she stares up at me. How her declaration of love gets cut off as her climax slams into her. The utter perfection of how she feels pulsing around me.

"*Fuck*, you feel so good." I brush the hair back from her face, kiss her slow and deep as I continue the unhurried rocking into her. "Think you've got more in you?"

She breathes out a laugh, then wraps her hand around my neck and tugs me down. "I think you'll probably make sure I do."

"Damn right I will. You better hang on, baby," I say, then thrust into her fast and hard, just like she asked me to earlier. Her increasing moans only spur me on more. "We're gonna see how many times I can make you come your first night as my wife. Any guesses?"

Her answer is cut off as I reach down and press my thumb to her clit, her body bowed off the bed as she comes again. How fucking lucky am I that this is my life? That I've now got this amazing, strong, brave, confident, independent woman to call mine? The thought and the way her body feels around me hurtles me straight toward my climax, and I thrust deep, spilling myself inside her, her name a groan on my lips.

Who would've thought a chance encounter at a shitty bar two years ago would lead to this? That a douchebag with grabby hands would be the catalyst for finding the love of my life? And that I get to spend the rest of my life showing her every day exactly what that means.

"Mine," I whisper into her neck, unable to keep the thought to myself.

She runs her hands down my back, then presses her lips to my ear. "Yours."

EPILOGUE

Many years later

winter

SEVENTY-SIX DAYS.

The number repeats over and over in my head, the rhythm matching Noah's heartbeat.

Seventy. Six.

Seventy. Six.

Days have a totally different meaning now. They're endless and too fast all at once. They are everything I've been terrified of my entire life, and yet they're everything that makes me happy.

It's not just the days that have a different meaning, though. *Life* has a totally different meaning now. I never thought I'd be here, and the change didn't happen overnight. Even after our wedding, there were issues I fought. But I learned to fight them *with* Cade, not against him. Seeing my name on his finger, peeking out from under his titanium wedding band, was a constant reminder that he found in me exactly what I found in him.

A home.

It's three in the morning, and we're lying in bed, our son nursing while Cade spoons me from behind, his lips pressed against my shoulder as he keeps constant eyes on Noah. His hand engulfs the baby's head, his thumb rubbing soft circles over downy brown hair.

"Maybe tomorrow he'll decide to go through the night." Cade's voice is deep with sleep, rasping out in a low rumble.

I look down at Mister Every Three Hours Like Clockwork and smile, running a finger down his cheek. "Somehow I doubt it."

Cade brushes his lips across my shoulder. "You know, I can feed him the milk you've pumped. You don't have to get up every night."

"I don't mind." And I don't. I just don't know how to explain it to Cade. How to put into words the bond I feel every time I hold our child in my arms. Every time I look into his eyes. Every time his finger grasps mine. How, even though I'm dead tired, I actually *enjoy* these middle of the night wake-up calls, when everything is silent and still and it's just the three of us in this tiny cocoon of ours.

My whole life, I've been scared of what it would mean

if I ever became a mom. Of how I could handle it. How I could actually do the job when I never had a role model worth anything.

How could I ever be a mom when my own didn't want to stick around long enough to be one to me?

Finding out I was pregnant was the second scariest day of my life, inching only slightly behind the day we brought Noah home from the hospital. I didn't understand how the doctors and nurses were just going to let me go home with this perfect little package, all seven pounds, fourteen ounces of him. Didn't they know my mom was a screw up? That *I* was a screw up who knew exactly nothing about being a mom? About taking care of a living, breathing human being?

Somehow, though, we've managed.

We've stumbled through, Cade and I adjusting to our new normal. And that was what was so refreshing to me. Knowing that even though he helped with Haley when she was born, *this*—being a parent for the first time, the bone-deep terror mixing with the overwhelming love that fills every ounce of your body—was as new to him as it was to me.

I realized very early on that I didn't have to compensate for the horrible person my mother was. It was the revolving issue that haunted me through most of my relationship with Cade. Like somehow I was predisposed to be just like her because we shared the same DNA.

That couldn't be further from the truth.

Despite the terror at finding out I was pregnant, I've

loved Noah since he was just an announcement on a tiny plastic stick. I loved him through every obstetrician appointment, through every ultrasound. Through every late-night bout of munchies, every kick to the bladder and knee to the ribs. I loved him even before I met him, and it was that thought that kept me going, even when I was terrified.

Later, after Noah's finished eating and is burped and changed, Cade asks, "You want me to take him back to his room?"

"In a minute," I say, and snuggle back into Cade's warm and comforting arms, which he wraps tighter around me, his lips finding mine even in the dark.

It's been seventy-six days since I heard our baby's first cry. Since I felt his skin on mine, looked into his eyes, touched his tiny toes. Since my life was turned upside down.

It's been seventy-six days since Cade and I brought a child into the world. And for once, I'm not counting down, but counting forward.

I can't wait to see what day seventy-seven brings.

————

THANK YOU FOR READING *OUR LOVE UNHINGED*! Want more swoons and steamy sexy times? Check out *Second Chance Charmer* when bad boy Finn returns to town after fleeing Havenbrook—and his first love Willow—without a word ten years prior.

OTHER TITLES BY BRIGHTON WALSH

HOLIDAYS IN HAVENBROOK SERIES

Main Street Dealmaker

HAVENBROOK SERIES

Second Chance Charmer

Hometown Troublemaker

Pact with a Heartbreaker

Captain Heartbreaker

Small Town Pretender

RELUCTANT HEARTS SERIES

Caged in Winter

Tessa Ever After

Paige in Progress

Our Love Unhinged

STAND-ALONE TITLES

Dirty Little Secret

Season of Second Chances

Plus One

ACKNOWLEDGMENTS

This book was my Mt. Everest, even in its shortened length. After months of nothing but blank documents staring back at me, every single one of these these twenty-five thousand words felt like the biggest accomplishment. Yay! I didn't forget how to write!

Going back and visiting the gang of the Reluctant Hearts series was bittersweet, because I knew going in, this novella would be the end. Even so, it was so rewarding, especially to see the characters come full circle. And while goodbye is always hard, it was time.

OLU wouldn't have been possible without the help of a few. I'm one of those lucky souls who've found their tribe, and there's no way I could do any of this without them.

To Christina, my Plot Whisperer, idea bouncer, cheap psychiatrist, cheerleader, supporter, and one of my very best friends. Thank you for putting up with my crazy and loving me in spite of it. I have no idea where I'd be without you.

To Ellis Leigh, for being my girls' night partner in crime and always being up for a glass of wine, some good food, and plannergasms. Thank you for holding my hand through all this crazy SP business. I don't even want to *think* about what kind of fumbles I would've made without you guiding me. Can't wait for World Domination.

To Jeanette Grey, the one who's been with me from the beginning—not just the beginning of the Reluctant Hearts series (thanks for telling me *Caged in Winter* wasn't a pile, btw), but from The Beginning. Eight years is a long time, and I'm so thankful we get to traverse this crazy-amazing adventure together.

To my editor Ashley for turning this around in no time and for wanting to put Winter in your pocket just as much as I do. Thanks for making my words shine.

To all my amazing readers out there who love these characters as much as I do, thank you. From the bottom of my heart. I wouldn't be here without your unwavering support.

To the bloggers who've supported me since *Caged in Winter* released, thank you a million. Special thanks to Becca, Candy, Cezanne, Christina, Funmbi, Hannah, Jaime, Jessica, Juliana, Kim, Michelle, Stacee, Valerie, and Heroes & Heartbreakers for helping to announce this super secret release.

Finally, to my guys, who continue to put up with my... eccentricities. Thank you for showing me every day how to live and love.

ABOUT THE AUTHOR

Award-winning *USA Today* and *Wall Street Journal* best-selling author Brighton Walsh spent a decade as a professional photographer before taking her storytelling in a different direction and reconnecting with her first love—writing. She likes her books how she likes her tea—steamy and satisfying—and adores strong-willed heroines and the protective heroes who fall head over heels for them. Brighton lives in the Midwest with her real life hero of a husband, her two kids—both taller than her—and her dog who thinks she's a queen. Her boy-filled house is the setting for dirty socks galore, frequent dance parties (okay, so it's mostly her, by herself, while her children look on in horror), and more laughter than she thought possible.

www.brightonwalsh.com
brighton@brightonwalsh.com

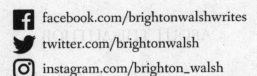

facebook.com/brightonwalshwrites

twitter.com/brightonwalsh

instagram.com/brighton_walsh

CPSIA information can be obtained
at www.ICGtesting.com
Printed in the USA
LVHW091318090422
715715LV00022B/2755

9 781685 180195